John Creasey – Master Storyteller

Born in Surrey, England in 1908 into a poor family in which there were nine children, John Creasey grew up to be a true master story teller and international sensation. His more than 600 crime, mystery and thriller titles have now sold 80 million copies in 25 languages. These include many popular series such as *Gideon of Scotland Yard*, *The Toff*, *Dr Palfrey* and *The Baron*.

Creasy wrote under many pseudonyms, explaining that booksellers had complained he totally dominated the 'C' section in stores. They included:

> Gordon Ashe, M E Cooke, Norman Deane, Robert Caine Frazer, Patrick Gill, Michael Halliday, Charles Hogarth, Brian Hope, Colin Hughes, Kyle Hunt, Abel Mann, Peter Manton, J J Marric, Richard Martin, Rodney Mattheson, Anthony Morton and Jeremy York.

Never one to sit still, Creasey had a strong social conscience, and stood for Parliament several times, along with founding the One Party Alliance which promoted the idea of government by a coalition of the best minds from across the political spectrum.

He also founded the British Crime Writers' Association, which to this day celebrates outstanding crime writing. The Mystery Writers of America bestowed upon him the Edgar Award for best novel and then in 1969 the ultimate Grand Master Award. John Creasey's stories are as compelling today as ever.

The Toff Series

A Bundle for the Toff
A Doll for the Toff
A Knife for the Toff
A Mask for the Toff
A Rocket for the Toff
A Score for the Toff
Accuse the Toff
Break the Toff
Call the Toff
Double for the Toff
Feathers for the Toff
Follow the Toff
Fool the Toff
Hammer the Toff
Here Comes the Toff
Hunt the Toff
Introducing the Toff
Kill the Toff
Leave It to the Toff
Kiss the Toff
Model for the Toff
Poison for the Toff
Salute the Toff
Stars for the Toff
Terror for the Toff
The Kidnapped Child
The Toff Among the Millions
The Toff and Old Harry
The Toff and the Crooked Copper
The Toff and the Deadly Parson
The Toff and the Deep Blue Sea
The Toff and the Fallen Angels
The Toff and the Golden Boy
The Toff and the Great Illusion
The Toff and the Lady
The Toff and the Runaway Bride
The Toff and the Sleepy Cowboy
The Toff and the Spider
The Toff and the Stolen Tresses
The Toff and the Toughs
The Toff and the Terrified Taxman
The Toff and the Trip-Trip-Triplets
The Toff at Butlins
The Toff at the Fair
The Toff Breaks In
The Toff Goes On
The Toff Goes to Market
The Toff in New York
The Toff in Town
The Toff in Wax
The Toff Is Back
The Toff on Board
The Toff on Fire
The Toff Proceeds
The Toff Steps Out
The Toff Takes Shares
Vote for the Toff

Murder Out of the Past (short stories)
The Toff on the Trail (short stories)

Salute the Toff

John Creasey

Copyright © 1941 John Creasey Literary Management Ltd.
© 2014 House of Stratus

All rights reserved. No part of this publication may be reproduced, stored in a retrieval system, or transmitted, in any form, or by any means (electronic, mechanical, photocopying, recording, or otherwise), without the prior permission of the publisher. Any person who does any unauthorised act in relation to this publication may be liable to criminal prosecution and civil claims for damages.

The right of John Creasey to be identified as the author of this work has been asserted.

This edition published in 2014 by House of Stratus, an imprint of Stratus Books Ltd., Lisandra House, Fore Street, Looe, Cornwall, PL13 1AD, U.K.
www.houseofstratus.com

Typeset by House of Stratus.

A catalogue record for this book is available from the British Library and the Library of Congress.

ISBN 07551-3627-6
EAN 978-07551-3627-8

This book is sold subject to the condition that it shall not be lent, resold, hired out, or otherwise circulated without the publisher's express prior consent in any form of binding, or cover, other than the original as herein published and without a similar condition being imposed on any subsequent purchaser, or bona fide possessor.

This is a fictional work and all characters are drawn from the author's imagination. Any resemblance or similarities to persons either living or dead are entirely coincidental.

Chapter One

The Toff At Ease

The Toff – or the Honourable Richard Rollison – was walking one day in July through the glades of the New Forest when he came upon a small village which he knew well, a quiet and secluded place. A small village green whereon the cricket pitch was still marked and wired off to prevent the cows from grazing on it, a single High Street with small terraces of thatch-roofed cottages, white walls and dark oak beams and facings, each with a narrow strip of well-tended garden in front of it. There nasturtium and antirrhinum, rambler and creeper, those lovely humble flowers of incredible colour, grew in abundance. There the windows were polished so that they reflected the slanting rays of a warm sun without showing long and irregular smears. Windows and doors were open, as if in silent invitation for the wayfarer to pass in and not pass by; curtains of lace, and sometimes chintz, moved gently in a breeze that robbed the evening of its true heat. A farm cart rumbled past; and a gnarled old man with a face tanned deep brown touched his forelock and wished the Toff good night.

"Good night," said the Toff, and he smiled, which was always a pleasing thing to see. He was at ease in an open-necked shirt and slacks, and his brown face glistened a little because of the warmth and his exertions. "You'll find the hay early this year, won't you?"

"Ar, that un be," said the old one.

The Toff would have passed on but for a cry from within a cottage that was standing in a small garden of its own, a charming place both colourful and clean.

"Rolly! Rolly, it can't be—wait a minute, wait!"

And as he turned, his eyes lighting up, a young woman came from the cottage, wrestling with a small apron that helped to cover a printed cotton frock, but did nothing to spoil a lively, lovely face and a figure which it did men good to see. Dark hair, tumbled as she pulled off the apron, set an oval face in a halo that seemed to have been born for it.

"Rolly, it *is* you!"

"Fay," said the Toff, with unfeigned pleasure, "it's good to see you."

He went inside, and drank tea, and watched the lovely Fay in the small lounge with its oak beams and its charm. The cottage suited her: it was the background she should have had. Odd that she had gone there only at the strong appeal of her husband, who was in Cyprus. The marriage would not have taken place but for the activity of the Toff.

As Fay talked the Toff recalled their story and the fact that the Draycotts (as they are now) had played a part in one of his adventures that he would never forget. There had been tragedy in it, and death; but there had also been hope and inspiration.

For the Toff it had started one day when he had been at his ease in London.

* * *

There were many who called the Hon. Richard Rollison a man-about-town, and they meant the term disparagingly. They said that he did not know what it was to do a fair day's work, that he was a drone with far more money than was good for him, and if they heard rumours of some of his activities they turned up their aristocratic noses and declared that for a man of his birth and breeding such notoriety was disgraceful.

They did not know of the legend which had grown up about Rollison in the East End of London, where his soubriquet of 'the Toff' was first inspired, and they turned a deaf ear to the reputation which slowly built about him, until he was as well known in the West End as the East. They would have laughed derisively had they been told that he took crime seriously, and even crusaded against it, for was it not a fact that he would spend weeks at a time east of Aldgate Pump? Was it not also true that even when he was at his Gresham Terrace flat, perhaps entertaining relatives of considerable complacency or, as they liked to say, importance, peculiar little men in ill-fitting clothes and with unbearable accents called to see him? Men, it was whispered, who had been in prison, or ought to have been, thieves and pick-pockets and probably far worse, and women too, with excessive rouge and lip-stick and with absurdly high-heeled shoes.

Yet the Toff was always very much the same, quick to smile and quiet-voiced, lazy to look at despite his seventy-two inches and his lean and well-proportioned figure. The smile was the real trouble, it was said, for he always created the impression that he was laughing at his guests, or else at some joke which he could or would not share: and socially each alternative was a crime.

One late afternoon early in September renowned for its perfect weather the Toff saw five distant relatives to his door and returned to his lounge, where Jolly was opening the windows.

"Thank the Lord," said the Toff, "that we needn't have another of those for a month, Jolly. Can you tell me why they must be at all?"

Jolly, inches shorter than the Toff, grey and sparse of hair, miserable of countenance although optimistic of temperament, with a lined face and a baggy patch under his chin which suggested that he had once been fat, allowed himself to say: "They are considered a duty, sir."

"Yes, I know," said the Toff. "But why should a group of back-biting old hypocrites continue to descend on me and vent their disapproval? Why don't they leave me alone?"

"Yes, sir," said Jolly, and moved slowly to the door. "Your good nature prevents you from making that *quite* clear, sir."

"Oh," said the Toff, and he looked surprised. "You needn't go, Jolly. Sit down."

"Thank you, sir." Jolly did not perch himself on the edge of a chair, but sat down and became comfortable, for the Toff had insisted on that long since. Moreover, the Toff rarely talked to him for the sake of talking: more often than not there would be some information or some problem he wanted to discuss.

Somewhat unexpectedly the Toff said: "Jolly, I'm tired."

"I'm sorry to hear that, sir," said Jolly. "I had thought that the recent period of inaction allied to a sequence of quite early nights would have the opposite effect."

"Yes I suppose so," said the Toff, "but I yawned twenty-one times between four o'clock and half past five."

"The company may have been the cause of that, sir."

"It was more than the company. It was boredom that started a long time before four o'clock today. London is empty, Jolly."

"This part of London, sir, perhaps."

"So little entertainment," said the Toff.

"Precisely, sir. Since Madame Litinov—"

"Never mention her name," said the Toff firmly. "And don't try to wish feminine company on me. I have finished with ballerinas for the time being. And film stars. And all the others. I am tired of exoticism; I want freshness, English charm, genuine vivacity that isn't ladled out with a spoon. Night-clubs and bad music are sickening me, while there is a remarkable inertia in the East End."

"For which we should be thankful, sir."

"Don't be sonorous," said the Toff, and he crossed one leg over the other. "I've been giving it some thought, and I think that a week or two in the country, on our own, might be a help. So you will drive down to the New Forest and see what you can find in the way of a small place, furnished not too hideously, and with an acre or two of its own ground. We will rusticate, Jolly."

"Very good, sir. Shall I go tonight?"

"As ever was," said the Toff. "You'll be down there by nine o'clock, and you can start looking round in the morning, Not a large place,

Jolly: one that you can look after without help from the locals, but one with a telephone and electric light."

"I know precisely what you want, sir."

"Good," said the Toff. "Then find it."

Jolly was on his way within half an hour, and the Toff wondered whether it had been a wise decision, played with the idea of going out for the evening, but put on slacks and a flannel jacket before settling down for an evening's reading. He was deep in a disquieting book by William Golding when the front-door bell rang.

He finished a paragraph, put the book down, and opened the door without giving much thought to the likely identity of his caller. It was still daylight, and there was a window in the passage which illuminated the Toff's front door excellently, and so enabled him to see the girl who stood there.

He had never seen her before.

She was neither tall nor short, and she was dressed in a light-grey costume with a white silk blouse that had frills at the V neck. A small hat covered dark hair, and it entered the Toff's mind that he was seeing what he had told Jolly he wanted to see: someone fresh and yet quite lovely, with wide-set blue eyes, a short nose and a short upper lip, a square chin which was the least bit shiny, and a complexion in which artifice had helped nature and not covered it.

"Good evening," said the Toff.

"Good evening. Is Mr.—Rollison in, please?"

"Yes," said the Toff. "I am Rollison."

"Oh," she said, and she almost looked disappointed, while before she could stop herself the words came: "I expected an older man, I'm sorry."

"Why be sorry?" asked the Toff. "And why stand there?" He stood aside for her to pass, and he saw that although she was self-possessed up to a point she looked about her quickly, while he fancied that the colour on her cheeks was partly due to excitement.

"And now," said the Toff, "don't apologise for calling, don't assure me that you know I'm busy, but if I could spare you a little time you'd be grateful. I have positively nothing to do, and I am very bored. Does that help?"

She smiled, quickly, gratefully.

"It does, a lot. I—I wouldn't have known of you, but a friend suggested that you might help, and I'm worried. My—my employer has disappeared, Mr. Rollison. He has been missing for two days, and I'm sure that something is wrong. May I tell you the whole story?"

The Toff pulled up a chair for her and said: "You certainly may."

Chapter Two

One Man Missing

She told her story with commendable brevity, her only preamble being that her name was Gretton, Fay Gretton, and that her employer owned a small estate agency which he ran under his own name of Draycott. She had been working for Draycott less than a month, but during that time she had seen nothing unusual. He was quite young – no more than thirty, she thought – and was engaged.

That had considerable bearing on the problem.

"He is planning to get married in ten days' time," said Fay Gretton earnestly, "and he's been working all hours to get the office work up to date so that he can leave it for a fortnight. That's why I'm so sure he would have been in if it had been possible."

"Go on," urged the Toff.

"I've called at his flat and telephoned him several times. He hasn't been there since Monday evening, and it's Wednesday now. I—" Fay hesitated, and then went on quickly: "I asked his fiancée whether she had heard from him, and she said no."

The Toff tapped the ash from his cigarette and asked: "And the lady wasn't perturbed?"

"No, not particularly. Apparently Mr. Draycott often goes away for two or three days at a time on business, and sometimes doesn't tell her—she is away quite a lot too. She told me," went on Fay, "that she thought I was making a lot of fuss about nothing."

"Too bad." The Toff's eyes were smiling.

Fay said sharply: "I hope you don't agree! I—oh, I'm sorry!"

"Don't be," said the Toff. "Let me get the essentials straight. Mr. Draycott was in business on Monday, returned to his flat that evening, and has not been seen since. The flat has been searched—"

"No," said Fay quickly. "I couldn't get in, and there's no one on the premises with a key. The people in the flat below said they heard him go out on Monday, and someone else said he was carrying a small attaché-case. But I can't be sure that the flat is empty, and—" She hesitated, and then went on with a rush: "I'm scared."

By that time the Toff had formed a judgment of Fay, mostly in her favour.

He imagined that she was about twenty-five, that she had spent several years in business, and that she would be capable. She would be unlikely to have inhibitions or obsessions: probably she was as mentally healthy as she was physically. He would not be surprised to learn that she had grown to think more of Draycott than a secretary should.

And from there, thought the Toff, the next step should have been easy. She was in love, and scared by things which were mostly imaginary. The fiancée's attitude suggested that was true, and yet the Toff found it hard to believe.

He said: "All right, Miss Gretton, we'll have a look at the flat for the sake of our peace of mind."

"You mustn't go to the police," she said quickly.

"I didn't propose to, but why not?"

"Well." She hesitated, and then smiled nervously. "If there was nothing the matter, and Mr. Draycott found that I'd had the police in the flat, it might cost me my job. Especially after Miss Harvey has scoffed at the idea of trouble. I've really no business to interfere, but—" She broke off, and the Toff finished for her: "He was so busy clearing up that you can't believe he would have gone off willingly without a word? That's reasonable enough, provided he's not temperamental."

"Great Scott, no! He's the sanest man I've met Do you know Ted Harrison?"

"I don't recall him," answered the Toff.

"He said you wouldn't," said Fay. "He's a part-time journalist—he really doesn't do much work—and he plays a lot of cricket. I've known him for years, and I happened to meet him at lunch-time. He knows Mr. Draycott well—he got me the job. I told him part of the story, and he said that it would be the kind of thing to interest you." Fay put her head to one side, and went on slowly: "He said so much about you that I thought you must be fifty at least to have crammed it all in."

"The talkative Mr. Harrison probably gave you many wrong impressions," said the Toff. "But I'm glad he sent you. If there's nothing to worry about, it's all right, and if there is we haven't lost much time."

"No," she said. "Ted—Ted said that you wouldn't laugh. It does seem pretty flimsy on the surface, doesn't it?"

"Well," said the Toff judicially, "I've known flimsier starts to major problems, and I've known cases that seemed all-important fade after twenty-four wasted hours. But rid your mind of all that the talkative Mr. Harrison said—by the way, has he got a nice-looking on-drive?"

"Yes," said Fay. "And he's pretty safe with the hook-shot."

"Then I do know him. You seem to know enough about cricket to talk in the vernacular, Fay."

"I used to go about with Ted a lot," she said.

"He's a tall and gloomy-looking gentleman with glasses and a spindly frame. Right?"

"Perfect!"

"A deep voice, perpetual complaints, and a passion for all things cricketing," added the Toff. "Well, the unexpected is often happening, and I certainly did not expect a mystery from Ted Harrison. Are you ready?"

She looked startled.

"For what?"

"For Draycott's flat."

"But—but how are you going to get in?"

The Toff, stepping towards his bedroom, looked at her over his shoulder with so comical an expression that she had to laugh. He did not tell her that into his pocket he had slipped a knife which had as one of its blades a pick-lock that had not yet failed him on ordinary locks, together with an interesting instrument with which to get past a Yale.

She had heard vaguely of the Toff, remembering the occasional mornings when the headlines of the popular Press told a story in which he figured. She had thought little of it, for to her it had seemed that he was a dilettante of crime about whom the Press had woven a legend. But now that she had seen him she found that her opinion was altered. There was at once something unassuming and reassuring about him, something suggesting that the mystery was the simplest thing to solve. He had not scoffed, nor thrown doubts, nor given her to believe that she was making mountains where there were none. In fact he had taken her visit and her story in his stride.

He was absurdly good-looking, of course, and it would have been easy to imagine him indolent. The appointments and the furniture of the flat bespoke wealth, which often went with laziness. Yet, if Ted Harrison had told the truth, he cared little for luxury.

She put that thought aside, for he led her downstairs and into Gresham Terrace. His flat, on the top floor of No. 55, was on a corner, and round the corner was a row of garages from which he took a Bristol. He did not seem to hurry, and did everything in leisurely fashion, but they were soon on the road to Chelsea. Draycott lived near the river.

Sitting next to the Toff, Fay told him that she had several times visited the flat in the evenings, to help to get the work cleared up. It was a small one, consisting of a small bedroom, a tiny kitchen, but one large studio room which would be freezing in the winter, but was cool and airy in the warmer months. The house itself, a large one, had long since been converted into six flats. Most of the tenants were artists. "Really artists?" asked the Toff.

"Well, I've only seen one or two of them, and they dress the part." They reached 14 Grey Street in less than fifteen minutes. It was one of a long row of terraced houses, tall and narrow, dowdy and grey, with the woodwork mostly in need of paint, and few of the windows really clean. Drab lace curtains, turned yellow with age, were at many front windows, and outside several of the houses were notices of apartments to let or offers of board-residence at moderate charges. It was neither impressive nor particularly depressing, and to the Toff the most homely sound was the hoot of a siren as a tug or a small cargo-boat passed along the Thames, some hundred yards from the end of the thoroughfare. The Toff pulled up and opened the door for her. "I don't know what Mr. Draycott would say," she said a little uncertainly.

"He needn't know," said the Toff. "And certainly you played no part in it, beyond telling me you were concerned for the gentleman, which should please him."

"Why?" asked Fay.

"Well," said the Toff easily, "it would please me." The hall of the house was dark.

From one of the flats a radio blared, and in another someone was making a hash of a Bach prelude. The stairs creaked noisily. One piece of the balustrade was broken, and he caught his hand on a splinter and winced. Together they reached the top landing. That was as large as the hall, and there were two flats – with Draycott's on the right-hand side. From the door on the left came the sound of men's voices.

The Toff glanced at the lock of Draycott's door and said: "Fay, look hard at the other flat, and warn me if the handle turns."

She turned her back to him as she obeyed, and the Toff opened his knife with the pick-lock, for the lock in front of him was old-fashioned, and would be the work only of a moment with that tool. He felt the end of the skeleton key bite at the lock, manipulated for some seconds, and then felt the barrel go back. He turned the handle and pushed the door open.

"I won't be a moment," he said, and stepped through, while Fay continued to stare at the door of the flat opposite. He saw the long, lofty studio with the big north-light set in the ceiling. It was furnished without taste and at little expense, but he was not interested in the furniture nor the size of the room. He half-closed the door behind him, and stood still, staring towards a couch in one corner.

Lying full length on it was a man, the face so mottled and distorted that it was unlikely that he was alive.

Chapter Three

Fast Work

The Toff stepped across to the couch and the motionless body, which was dressed in a dark-grey lounge suit, and looked to be that of a youngish man. He disliked the thought of Fay Gretton making this discovery, and stayed no longer than was necessary to confirm that the man had been dead for some time; the flesh of his hand was cold.

About his neck was a nylon stocking, drawn tight.

That explained the purple mottle of his face, the protruding eyes, and the swollen lips, which the tongue pushed a little aside. It was not a nice sight. The Toff turned away, but then went back, drawing on his right-hand glove and slipping his hand into the man's breast pocket. He drew out a wallet, and inside it was a letter addressed to

James Draycott Esq.,
14 *Grey Street, Chelsea, S.W.*

The Toff replaced the letter and the wallet, examined the stocking at the man's neck, and saw that it had been drawn tight, but that there were no marks of fingers or thumbs on the swollen neck. That suggested that the noose had been slipped over, probably while the man had been sitting on the settee.

There was no sign of a struggle.

The Toff drew off his glove and returned to the door. A man whom he had not known, and not heard of until that day, had been murdered, and the Toff was too hardened to death in all its forms to be worried by that. But his concern for the girl outside was the greater because of her obvious feeling for Draycott.

She was still watching the opposite door.

From his expression there was nothing to learn.

"Is it empty?" she asked.

"Up to a point," said the Toff. "There isn't a key of this flat at the office, is there?"

"No, I told you." She looked alarmed. "Why?"

"Because we need one," said the Toff, "and I'll have to get one made, or ..." He hesitated, and she asked in a sharp voice: "What have you found in there?"

"Fay," said the Toff very quietly, "I want you to stay here again for just two minutes. I'll tell you then." He smiled. "A bet?"

She nodded, and the Toff slipped back into the room. He found the key which he should have taken before in the hip pocket of the man lying there, and rejoined the girl. She had lost most of her colour, and her eyes were very bright.

"Is he all right?" she demanded.

"I would give a lot for a comfortable settee, and an armchair for you," said the Toff, "but I think you can take bad news, Fay. He's dead. He has been killed."

She stood very still, staring at him with her eyes wide, yet slowly changing their expression, as if the news did not sink in at once. Her body kept quite rigid, and he saw that her hands began to clench. Then her breathing grew heavy.

"Oh, no!" she said, and her voice was low-pitched. "Oh, it can't be true!"

The Toff said nothing, and she looked towards the door, as if determined to go in and see for herself. He meant to prevent that, but he did not have to fight, for she shivered from head to foot, then turned towards the stair-head.

The Toff closed and locked the door, slipped the key into his pocket – handling the key with his gloves so as to make sure that his finger-prints did not show – and took the girl's arm as she began to descend the stairs. She walked stiffly, as if with no idea of what she was doing. As they reached the landing a door opened and a woman appeared.

The Toff saw her clearly.

She was very tiny and very smart – not characteristic of that part of Chelsea, nor in a flat of that kind, for she had spent a small fortune on her dress. Her hair was red, and the most remarkable thing about her were her eyes, very large and brilliant, and amber in colour.

She looked curiously at the girl and the Toff, then preceded them down the stairs.

"That might be unfortunate," the Toff said *sotto voce,* and to his mingled surprise and relief Fay said: "Oughtn't we to have been seen?"

"It doesn't matter a great deal." He had spoken to try to make her think of something else. "We'll manage, Fay. Bundle in."

"But what are you going to do?"

"I'll handle it all," said the Toff quietly. "That's one thing you needn't let yourself worry about"

She said: "Thank God I came to you."

Then she stepped into the car, and he followed her, driving more quickly on the return journey. She did not ask questions when he reached the flat, and after he had insisted that she should drink a weak whisky-and-soda, which made her grimace, but brought some colour back to her cheeks, he telephoned a Kensington number.

A pleasant feminine voice answered: "Who is calling, please?"

"Anthea," said the Toff quietly, "can you desert Jamie for a few hours, perhaps even a day or so?"

"Can I—*what!*"

"I'm quite serious, and I'm not alone," said the Toff.

"Oh, Rolly, nothing's the matter, is it? Yes, I'll come over. Jamie can look after himself. What—what is it?"

"I'll tell you when you get here," said the Toff.

He replaced the receiver, to find Fay staring at him, neither blankly nor with excessive curiosity.

"Who was that?"

"A friend of mine who'll be a friend of yours."

"I see," Fay said. "You're very kind."

"Nonsense," said the Toff, and took up the receiver again. He saw no purpose in trying to hide the necessary formalities: to try to enshroud her with a cloak of hush-hush would do more harm than good. So she heard him speak to Scotland Yard, and then to a Chief Inspector McNab, who also lived in Chelsea, and who had taken a well-earned day's rest.

To the Toff, McNab did not sound affable.

"What ees it, Rolleeson?" His accent was unreliable, and privately the Toff considered that he was a case of the Scotsman occasionally pretending to be what he was. "If there is any reason for a call the night—"

"Would I be worrying you otherwise?" asked the Toff reproachfully, to which McNab replied that he would not be surprised. He stopped his complaints when the Toff told him what had happened. He finished: "So the key's here, Mac, and I disturbed nothing."

"Will ye bring the key to the hoose?" demanded McNab.

"I'd rather you sent for it," said the Toff, "and I'll come to see you later." He was an old acquaintance of McNab.

There had been a time, particularly in the days when the Toff had been little known, and when legend had not grown up about him, when his methods and his habit of acting first and advising the police afterwards had caused trouble with McNab and others at the Yard. But today, if the police did not entirely approve of the means he used, they were prepared to acknowledge that he obtained results.

To this he responded by covering such breaches when it was possible; and they lived in peace, often working at one with each other.

It was some minutes after the Toff had spoken to McNab that a policeman called for the key, and the address. Less than five minutes later Anthea arrived.

The Toff had met her first as Lady Anthea Munro, but she was now married to her Jamie, a worthy Scotsman who worshipped her, and yet did not look askance at her friendship with the Toff, whose reputation was not what it might have been, and who was said to have had *affaires* with more lovelies in London than any other man. Jamie, being shrewd, probably suspected that those *affaires* were frequently no more than gossip.

There had been an affair of violence when Anthea had taken a keen if not active interest, and that had been the beginning of a friendship likely to last. And Anthea the right kind of common sense to help Fay Gretton. Fay would not be likely to talk to him about her feelings for Draycott; but she would talk to Anthea.

Anthea was twenty-seven, neither short nor tall, fair and blue-eyed and possessing a something which only the rugged moorland of Scotland can give to a woman. She took control of the situation with a speed which would have amused the Toff in different circumstances. He told her what had happened, while she looked at her face in a mirror and grimaced, and said: "There's a dreadful wind outside; look at my hair."

"Isn't it always untidy?" asked the Toff. "Thank *you*, sir. But may I use your bedroom to straighten it?"

"Use on," said the Toff, and Anthea looked at Fay with her head perched a little to one side. Fay stood up, without speaking, and went into the bedroom with the other woman. The Toff sat back to consider the situation.

Draycott, presumably, had been murdered at the flat.

That needed a motive.

He sat up abruptly.

Draycott had been about to marry another woman, and Fay Gretton had wished it otherwise. Could Fay have determined to stop it at all costs? Could that explain her persistence that Draycott was missing in peculiar circumstances? Could she have known of the death, and been unable to keep quiet?

The Toff tried to push the thought aside, but it was persistent. On the face of it there seemed no sense in believing that she had known Draycott to be dead when she had called at Gresham Street. But it *was* a possibility.

"Although," mused the Toff, "had the fiancée been the victim it would have been more logical. I think Fay will stand up to any suspicions, but McNab might get that great mind of his busy. I wonder how long it will be before he arrives? And should I go to Chelsea?"

He decided then that a second visit to Grey Street was advisable, and he was on his feet when the telephone rang. He answered it promptly, to hear an unfamiliar man's voice at the other end of the wire.

"Mr. Rollison, please."

"Speaking," said the Toff.

"Oh, it's you," said the man at the other end in a voice that suggested he had not received much pleasure. "I say, Rollison, have you had a visit from a Miss Fay Gretton?"

"Who are you?" asked the Toff.

"Oh, sorry. Harrison—Ted Harrison. We've met each other. Have you seen her?"

"It would be an idea if you came round," said the Toff. "Yes, she's here."

"What are you sounding mysterious about?" demanded Harrison, whose voice was deep and whose manner seemed irritable. "I can come round, although not for long. Why?"

"You'll see."

"Oh, all right," said Harrison gruffly. "I'll come. But you can set Fay's mind at rest meanwhile."

The Toff said, sharply: "*What?*"

"You can set her mind at rest. That's plain enough, isn't it?" demanded Harrison. "I had a call from Draycott half an hour ago. He's up North—he'd been called away on urgent business and couldn't get a message through before. I—*What* did you say?"

Chapter Four

Says Harrison

It was quite absurd.

For a moment – only for a moment – the Toff was taken off his balance, and his exclamation had understandably annoyed Harrison. But he recovered quickly, and he said sharply: "There's something wrong, all the same. Come round at once will you?"

Harrison rang off without answering.

The Toff felt irritated with him, and yet acknowledged that the man had some excuse.

The Toff waited for fifteen minutes, and during that time heard something that sounded like crying from the bedroom. Anthea was working the oracle; Fay could safely be left to her. Yet that peculiar suspicion – if it could be called a suspicion – persisted. Why had Fay been so insistent that something was wrong?

Could she have had prior knowledge?

The Toff was still wondering when the door-bell rang, and he admitted Harrison. He recognised the man immediately, although it was a year or more since they had played on opposite sides, and then they had been in flannels and had had little to say to each other. Before that, however, Harrison had frequently played against the Toff, who was a medium-paced bowler of some renown, and a batsman good enough for most first-class counties.

Tall and almost weedy, with an untidy mop of dark-brown hair, large horn-rimmed glasses, and a continually aggrieved expression on a homely, even pugnacious, face, Harrison walked with a stoop, and was the last man who would have been expected to be successful at any game. He was dressed in an old pair of flannels and a tweed jacket worn a little at the elbows, and was smoking a pipe that would soon become offensive. But his eyes were smiling behind his glasses; he was not the sourpuss that he liked to pretend.

"Hallo, Rolly—glad to see you."

"Thanks," smiled the Toff. "Having a good season?"

"Fair, thanks. You haven't been playing a lot, have you?"

"One way and the other, I've been busy," said the Toff, "but we needn't worry about that now. Are you sure about this message from Draycott?"

Harrison stared. "Of course I'm sure."

"Where did the call come from?"

"Manchester—the Queen's Hotel."

"That's something," said the Toff. To Harrison's surprise he put through a call to Draycott at the Queen's, Manchester. He was told there would be a ten-minute delay. So he sat on the edge of an easy chair, while Harrison stood with his back to the fireplace and regarded him with some perplexity.

"What *is* all this mystery about?"

"Draycott," said the Toff. "Did you recognise his voice?"

"I certainly did."

"With no possibility of mistake?"

"None at all. Rolly, don't keep hedging. What's the matter?"

"I'm hoping that there's been a case of mistaken identity." Rollison explained what had happened, and saw the other's face drop.

"Good Lord!" exclaimed Harrison. "I—you see what it implies, don't you?"

"You have a try," said the Toff.

Harrison licked his lips, and then began to refill his pipe.

"It's a crazy business all the way round," he said gruffly. "Draycott isn't the type to rush off like that without giving any notice at his office. He lives for the place, and he'd go crazy if he thought he didn't get in touch every day. But he shoves off like that, and leaves it two days before he gets in touch with me. It doesn't make sense."

"Well," said the Toff, "what does?"

Harrison gulped.

"You thought Draycott was dead, and you find a letter to him in the dead man's pocket. *Prima facie* evidence, all right But if Draycott's alive, who killed the man at his flat?"

"Precisely."

"You know," said Harrison, "I don't like it. But there does not seem any sense in his 'phoning me tonight. If he'd killed someone and tried to lose himself he wouldn't make a bloomer like that. Draycott's no fool."

"That's a point," agreed the Toff dryly. "What do you know about him?"

"I've known him since we were at school—Effingham—fifteen years ago now. Good sort, a useful bat, but more energetic than I'll ever be. He had an uncle in the estate business, and worked with him for a few years before the said uncle went broke. Draycott had a few thousand he could use, started his own business in the West End—a pretty plucky thing to do—and seemed to thrive. I know he's been a bit tight for money once or twice, but not for some years. His prospective father-in-law might have explained that—Old Man Harvey is pretty well lined."

"Do you know the girl?" asked the Toff.

"Slightly," said Harrison. "She's a bit prim and proper, but nice to look at. I shouldn't have thought she was Draycott's type, but you never can tell, and he seemed keen. The money," added Harrison quickly, "wouldn't have attracted Jimmy Draycott. I know there was quite a bit of opposition to a match before Harvey gave way. They've been engaged a whale of a time—five or six years, I suppose."

"Thanks," said the Toff. "That gives me the picture of Draycott I was after. I—"

The telephone rang, and he broke off to answer it. The operator told him that Mr. Draycott was not at the hotel, but that the operator would take a message if necessary. Yes, a Mr. Draycott *was* staying at the Queen's.

"Tell him, please, that Mr. Harrison is coming up to see him, by the night train, and is particularly anxious not to miss him. Will you do that?"

"Yes, sir."

"But—" began Harrison, only to find that the Toff was flashing the telephone, and before he could protest had obtained Euston Station Booking Office. He reserved two sleepers on the late train to the North, and replaced the receiver, turning to see Harrison's somewhat indignant gaze on him.

"But I'm not going up there! I'm playing tomorrow, and—"

"I hope you're not," said the Toff. "I hope we're both going to Manchester. I want Draycott properly identified."

Harrison said sharply: "You still think the message might have been a fake?"

"It's possible. Are you coming?"

"Oh, all right," said Edward Harrison, but although he showed no enthusiasm his eyes were bright.

It was then that the telephone rang again, and Harrison groaned.

"Oh, Lord I Will that thing ever stop?"

"In time," said the Toff, and he lifted the receiver, to hear McNab's voice. McNab had found everything as the Toff had said, and had come to the conclusion that the dead man was Draycott. Did he, the Toff, know anyone who could identify the body?

"I think you'd better get in touch with his family," said the Toff.

"There's none left," said Harrison in an urgent whisper. "The uncle died a year ago."

"Or his fiancée's family."

McNab wanted to know why the girl mentioned earlier would not do, and the Toff told him that she was too distraught to identify a body.

"Ye've told me *all* ye know, haven't ye?" demanded McNab.

"I certainly have," said the Toff mendaciously.

"Ye didna start this?"

"My dear Mac," said the Toff with every sign of testiness, "I had a call from a friend of a friend who told me Draycott was missing, and I offered to go along to the flat with the girl. I found what you found. The girl will be here—or," he added as an afterthought, "at 1023 Bayswater Road, with a Mr. and Mrs. Fraser. But give her a few hours' rest."

"What will ye be doing?"

"Sleeping, I hope," said the Toff.

There was little that McNab could want to see him about, except to confirm the circumstances in which the body had first been found, and there was no great hurry about that. There were the relatives and friends to find, and a thousand-and one routine items that would mean a sleepless night for the detective.

The Toff and Harrison, therefore, had the night to work in.

There was ample time for the train, and the Toff did not want to hurry Anthea or Fay; but within ten minutes of McNab's call Anthea came from the bedroom, and through the open door the Toff saw that Fay was sitting in front of the dressing-table combing her hair.

Anthea smiled.

"She'll be all right, Rolly. I'm taking her home for tonight, as she would normally be alone."

"Bless you," said the Toff.

He did not tell either woman of Harrison's news, for he was far from convinced that James Draycott was at Manchester, and unawareness would do Fay less harm than a new fear. Instead Rollison accompanied them to Anthea's car, and before they went off Fay gripped his hand firmly.

"You've been a great help, Rolly."

"I've done nothing."

"That's just it," said Fay, and she turned her head away quickly, while Anthea let in the clutch and drove towards the end of Gresham Terrace.

It was a fine, bright night, for the moon was nearly full and very clear, and he could see the people walking along the road – as well as the woman who was standing by a small car nearly opposite No. 55. He might not have thought twice about her but for the fact that a gust of wind made her grab her hat, and thus fixed his attention on her hair.

He walked past without a second glance, but as he went he was recalling that he had seen that small, red-haired woman at 14 Grey Street, Chelsea, and he did not think that it was a coincidence that she was outside his house.

Inside, he said to Harrison: "Go up to the flat and wait, will you? I'll be back in twenty minutes or so."

"Where are you going?" Harrison demanded testily. "And why *do* you have to make a lot of mystery?"

"It may be inherited vice," said the Toff, "or it may be forced on me. I wish you would stop behaving like the world's worst Jonah, and be a rational human being for once. I'll be back in twenty minutes or so, or I'll 'phone you." "All right," said Harrison.

"And if you could pack a few odds and ends," said the Toff, "it would help, my man being away." While Harrison was preparing to deliver a crushing rejoinder the Toff went again into the street. He turned right, towards Piccadilly, and the red-haired woman followed him.

Chapter Five

The Woman With Red Hair

The Toff afterwards said that it was the second glimpse of the woman with red hair that really caught his interest, and which first intimated that the case might be out of the ordinary. Until then he had imagined it to be a tale of personal tragedy, a crime of passion or even despair, without any of the ramifications likely to attract him. He was not interested in the murder of a man or woman as such; but when it was connected with a wider crime – that was a different matter. It was no part of his self-appointed task to harry individuals driven to a point of insanity by their immediate circumstances, and he did not propose to make it so. The red-haired woman made it very different. Even the Toff could hardly have said why, but from the moment she followed him he approached the mystery in a completely different mood.

He walked slowly, as if his sole purpose was to enjoy the night air, and when he reached Piccadilly he turned away from it at the first opportunity and strolled through those narrower thoroughfares which are traps for the unwary. He saw two girls walking together, and heard them speak to a man who was passing on the other side of the road. The man ignored them, but the Toff looked across the road, as if idly.

The woman with red hair, who had been no more than a few yards behind him since he had left the flat, quickened her pace. He heard her shoes clicking on the pavement, and he was not surprised when he heard her say: "Aren't you a bit bored, dear?" The Toff turned abruptly, as if startled. Not only the moon, but a street lamp, showed her clearly. She was, in a small-featured way, good-looking, and again he was astonished by her huge amber eyes. She did not look nervous, but her dress and her make-up did nothing to suggest that she had spoken to him in the way of business. "I'm all right, thanks," he said. "Go on with you," she scoffed, and he knew that she was acting a part. Her voice was low-pitched, but well-modulated. "Let's go for a little walk."

"We-ell …" said the Toff uncertainly.

He was genuinely surprised when she slipped an arm through his and urged him towards the end of the street. The two girls on the other side of the road stared, as if vindictively, while the red-haired woman went on: "It's miserable being alone, I know. I'm alone most of the time myself."

"I'm sorry about that," replied the Toff naïvely.

"Oh, well, it can't be helped," she said, and they walked for some hundred yards in silence. By then they had reached Piccadilly again, and were heading for Hyde Park Corner. "It's such a pity, too; I've a comfortable little flat in Park Lane."

"Have you really?"

He had expected mention of the flat, but had taken it for granted that she would say in Chelsea. Park Lane intrigued him, and he smiled down at her, as if he were beginning to realise that she had extended a tacit invitation. But he did nothing else to help her, although she pressed close to his side, a rather odd thing, for she did not reach his shoulder. But her left hand, cool and firm, gripped his wrist.

"Why don't you come along for a drink?" she suggested.

He might have imagined it, but he fancied that her breathing grew a little heavier, and he would not have been surprised to know that she was waiting on his answer with considerable anxiety.

"Well, that's nice of you, but wouldn't you rather go somewhere else for a change?"

"It wouldn't be so comfortable."

The Toff appeared to hesitate, but he did not turn away when they reached Park Lane. Some hundred yards along she turned into the driveway of a large new block of flats – flats, the Toff knew, which were extortionate in their rents, and where only the wealthy could hope to live.

"You're sure you don't mind?" he said with apparent diffidence.

"My dear, why should I?"

Her voice had altered, no longer in any way diffident nor anxious, but full and confident. A pleasing and cultured voice, with a slightly husky tone. The Toff looked down on her, and he could see that her profile was a lovelier thing than he had thought before. He said nothing else, but continued to behave like a naïve and ingenuous young man, smiling as if nervous when they reached the hallway of the flats and its brilliant light. She took him to a lift, which was self-operated, and they went up to the fourth floor.

"I'm so glad you decided to come," she said. "I get bored night after night on my own."

Nothing would really have surprised the Toff then.

He would have been faintly annoyed and also amused had he found that the long arm of coincidence – in which he had a considerable belief – had brought the red-haired woman to Gresham Terrace by accident, although the knowledge that she had been at Chelsea made that seem unlikely.

The woman opened the door with a key and pushed it.

The Toff stepped through into a small foyer, which led through an open door to a long, low-ceilinged lounge with wall lighting that had a softening and pleasing effect. The furniture was ultra-modern, most of the chairs of steel tubing, and there was a nest of tables.

The room was empty.

The red-haired woman closed the door, and then Rollison had the next intimation that she had not brought him here by chance. For she slipped the bolt home, quickly, and as though she hoped he would not notice it. He affected not to, but watched her when she turned round.

She was wearing a black two-piece, with a green blouse, and the combination suited her. Her tiny face was flawless, with the creamy skin that redheads so often have, and her eyes were huge.

Her teeth, when she smiled, looked perfect.

"Well, here we are," she said. "There's a drink in that cabinet. Do help yourself."

"I don't think I will just now," said the Toff. The woman's smile hardened for a moment, but she shrugged and laughed it off.

"Please yourself. By the way, shouldn't we exchange names?"

The Toff said carefully: "Well, I don't know, but I don't really mind. Mine's Rollison, Richard Rollison. What's yours?"

And then he knew that his first guess had been true.

She stared, her features hardening, and the smile disappeared from her lips. For some seconds she stood there, quite expressionless, except for a blaze of anger in her eyes, an anger which might have been tinged with fear. And then she snapped: "You *beast!*"

"Really!" said the Toff. She knew of him, obviously, but the fact that she had not recognised him proved that she had never seen him before. "We mustn't put it quite like that, Delilah. We were getting on so well," he added. His eyes were laughing, mocking her.

"You've made a mistake." She had to force the words out, and Rollison knew that she hardly knew what she was saying. And no one would be alarmed by him – or by his name – unless they possessed a guilty conscience. He was intrigued, but did not think her alarm was wholly assumed.

"What, another?" asked the Toff, and seemed genuinely amused. "If I believe all I hear I'm always making them, but I get over it. You brought me here to talk. Supposing you start, instead? There are gaps I would like filled in."

"*Gaps!*"

This was absurd, thought the Toff. She was hardly worth sharpening his sword against, and she was clearly frightened – unless, of course, she was putting up an act. He doubted that as he watched her breast rising and falling, and the tension in her amber eyes.

"You heard," he said. "I know Draycott was killed, and how, and almost who killed him. But I don't know why."

She said in a whisper it was hard to hear: "It's a lie! He wasn't killed; he- -"

"Myra, my dear!"

The voice came from one of the doors that the Toff had seen, but which had been closed a moment before. A man's voice, deep and not displeasing, and yet with a sharp note that made the woman swing round from the Toff and look towards the newcomer. The Toff simply glanced over his shoulder and waited for the man to come forward. And while he waited he sat on the arm of a settee.

He saw a man of a height with himself, very fair-haired, and in a ruddy, rugged way, handsome. His lips were very red, and his eyes a clear blue. His complexion was fresh-coloured, and a nose inclined to be pug-shaped was faintly tinged with red. The very fair eyebrows were raised, and the fair lashes seemed to emphasise the blueness of his eyes.

"Good evening," said the Toff.

"Good evening," said the newcomer urbanely. "Myra, my dear, you were getting too excited, which was hardly polite to your friend. Do I understand you are a Mr. Rollison?"

"You do," said the Toff, and as he appraised the man who approached him he knew that he was looking into the eyes of one who would fight ruthlessly. The Toff distrusted him even at a glance.

"My name is Lorne," said the fair-haired man.

"Delighted," said the Toff.

"My wife," went on Lorne earnestly, "is a somewhat highly strung woman who has peculiar ideas, Mr. Rollison. I'm sure that you hardly expected to find me here when you came, but I trust you will agree with me that the wise thing to do, and thus avoid a most awkward situation, would be for you to go. I assure you that I shall bear no malice."

"Nice of you," said the Toff amiably, "but I'm not sure that I want to go yet, Mr. Lorne. I—" he paused when Lorne's brows contracted, and the fleshy, red lips tightened. "But please don't get annoyed. You doubtless heard me mention a man named Draycott?"

"Draycott?—Draycott?—I don't remember."

The Toff was silent for a moment, and when he smiled there was a grimness in his eyes. He stood up, then sat in the chair instead of on it, took cigarettes from his pocket and lit one with exaggerated *sang-froid*. He closed his case and put out his cigarette-lighter.

"An interesting bluff, but I don't think we need carry it too far. You know quite well that your wife brought me here because both of you were wondering who had been to Draycott's flat. Probably she hoped to get the story out of me, when she had me drunk, but I'll give her the credit by saying that she didn't act her part as if she lived it."

"Don't talk nonsense that I don't understand," said Lorne. "I have apologised for my wife. Now be good enough to go."

The Toff stared at him, smoked for some seconds in silence, and then stood up. He looked at Myra Lorne – if Lorne was her name – and raised one brow above the other.

"You should be very careful," he warned. "You're too highly strung to be safe, and when the police ask questions they won't consider your nerves. Good night, Delilah, and thanks for breaking up my boredom."

He looked from her towards Lorne, and there was mockery in his smile. And then he turned towards the door, as if he had no anxiety and no thought other than going out. But as he turned he saw the stealthy movement that Lorne made towards his right-hand pocket.

The Toff reached the door, stretched out a hand for the knob, and then jumped to one side. He heard a sharp *zutt!* and a split-second later saw a bullet bury itself in the wood of the door. He did not stop moving, but picked up one of the tubular-steel tables and flung it at Lorne; and the man ducked, so that his second shot went wide.

Chapter Six

Night Train

Things happened so quickly that there seemed no measurable gap between the moment of starting and the moment of ending. Lorne's quick movement to avoid the table failed, and he was struck on the shoulder. He staggered, and the silenced automatic in his hand fell to the carpet. A third shot, released by the concussion, cut across the carpet and sent small pieces of fluff flying upwards, but it was well away from the Toff.

He went forward very quickly and picked up the gun.

He backed towards the door, covering the man and the woman, and pushing a hand through his hair as he went. He was smiling, but not amused. He saw Lorne rubbing at his shoulder, and saw the glitter in the man's blue eyes. He heard a gasp from the woman, and when he glanced at her could see that she was staring in horror and dread.

"Well, that's that," said the Toff without heat. "We do see life, don't we?"

Lorne said harshly: "Myra, keep your mouth shut!"

"Come," said the Toff, "that's no nice way to talk to a lady, and Myra probably feels she would like to get the thing off her conscience. All I want is to know why Draycott died. I could fill in the rest."

"You can't prove that anyone killed anyone, and if you're crazy enough to go to the police you won't get any satisfaction there."

Rollison said easily: "The shooting here *is* a criminal offence."

"Perhaps it is," said Lorne, and he drew a deep breath. The Toff admired his nerve, for he stepped to the walnut cabinet, opened it, and brought out a bottle of whisky. He poured out a finger and swallowed it neat, and then pushed the glass away from him.

"Better?" asked the Toff.

"Your damned words don't worry me," snapped Lorne. "You're making a mistake if you think you can use this against me. If you go to the police I shall say that I came home unexpectedly and found you with my wife. If you make a charge you'll get into the headlines in a different way from usual. Clear out, or I'll 'phone the police myself."

The Toff sat down on the edge of the settee again. He smoked in silence, regarding Lorne as he might have done a biological specimen under a microscope. At last: "I now have the measure of Mr. Lorne, Christian name unknown," he said. "Of the nasty things I've heard, that was one of the nastiest, but from Myra's point of view and not mine."

"*I'll* worry about her."

"Which is precisely what you don't seem likely to do," said the Toff; "but I suppose I can't help that. However, I'll meet you halfway. I won't go to the police yet, and you will keep your pretty little story for another day. Let it be understood," he added gently, "that I act out of consideration for Myra, not for myself. It suits me to let it pass."

"You damned liar!" said Lorne roughly. "You've been pushed into a corner."

"Suit yourself," said the Toff. "We're not getting anywhere. I'm interested chiefly in Draycott."

"I don't give a damn who you're interested in. Clear out!" He would not have welcomed scandal, but would not lose Lorne and the woman because of that. The fact was, he had nothing to use against either to implicate them in the murder of the man in Grey Street. To make a formal charge out of the present shooting without bringing proof of the strangling would defeat his own ends.

There was, moreover, the possibility that Lorne's story, supported by Myra, would be more convincing than the Toff's.

He said slowly: "We can almost call it stalemate, but for a very simple reason. Draycott was one of a series, of course, and I want more than proof of his murder. There are others involved, and I want them all. And so," he added, "I'll be back."

"You'll have to hurry," sneered Lorne.

"Oh, I'll come in my own good time," said the Toff, and he backed towards the door. He reached and opened it with his left hand, still covering the couple with the automatic. "For the gun," he said, "many thanks."

He went out.

He closed the door with a bang and moved quickly but heavily along the passage. He heard the door open again, but resisted a temptation to look round. It closed, and then he turned and went back, moving very swiftly but without a sound. He could hear a mutter of conversation inside the room, and when he went down on his knees, could hear the words coming through the gap at the bottom of the door.

Lorne was saying: "You damned little fool!"

"I—I was scared, Luke." The woman's voice was shaky.

"Next time you get scared, hold your tongue. You told him that we'd heard of him, and if you hadn't he wouldn't have known any different from what you tried to put over at first. God, you women!"

"I'm sorry; I lost my head."

"Sorry!" barked Lorne, and the Toff knew that he was working off not only his temper, but his fright. "I'll say you're sorry! Now we've got Rollison interested, and that's the one thing we were told not to do."

"I—I know."

There was a silence, broken by the chink of glass, and then the banging of a door. The man or the woman had left the room, while the Toff was straightening up considering the most important thing he had heard.

"Now we've got Rollison interested, and that's the one thing we were told not to do."

There were questions of importance arising, and they would have to be answered before he could get a clear picture of what was happening. He took a visiting-card from his pocket, one inscribed with his name and address. He took also a pencil, and in a few short lines drew on the reverse side of the card a top hat set at a rakish angle, a monocle with its string dangling, and a swagger-cane. He slipped the card through the letter-box of the flat, which was No. 81, and walked quietly away.

The card was typical of the Toff, one of those gestures which added melodrama to his adventures. It was difficult to explain just why he had started it, but long experience had told him that the cumulative psychological effect of similar cards was considerable, and in a way he worked on the psychological angle a great deal.

He was puzzled but not dissatisfied.

He made sure that he would not forget the doorway out of the block of flats, which were called Dring Mansions, and as he walked back towards Gresham Terrace he took particular care that he was not followed. The brilliant moon was helpful, and he was quite sure that he finished his journey alone. He let himself in with the key, and as he opened the door he heard a movement inside the room. Harrison was stepping towards the door. Rollison saw his relief, but Harrison scowled.

"I thought you said twenty minutes? You've been gone nearly an hour."

"Which is an exaggeration," said the Toff. "I've been less than forty minutes. But you haven't cooled down, I see." He grinned as he stepped past him to the telephone, and Harrison – behind the Toff's back – smiled. But aloud he complained: "Do you think all these telephone calls are necessary?"

"Great Scott, no!" said the Toff. "I like 'em."

He dialled a number, without saying that he was calling a certain public house in the Mile End Road. For the Mile End Road it was a pretentious establishment, with a saloon bar and a private bar, as well as the usual public and jug-and-bottle departments, while in the large shed at the back of it there was a place called:

'Bert's Gymnasium'

The Toff had first come across that gymnasium after watching a bout at the Ring, Blackfriars, and having a sharp disagreement with a would-be bilking bookmaker. His method of handling the bookmaker had so intrigued a large and barrel-shaped gentleman called by all and sundry 'Bert' that the Toff had been invited to 'come rahnd and 'ave one privit'. To which suggestion the Toff had agreed, and he had been introduced to the Mile Corner, by which the pub was known, and later to the gymnasium, where Bert trained or tried to train an amazing miscellany of would-be boxers. Old-timers who wanted exercise, present-day champions who needed to keep their muscles supple, and promising beginners who would otherwise have gone through the full horrors of the chopping-block stage were welcomed at the gymnasium. Bert, who owned the gym as well as the inn, was an ex-middleweight county champion, an honest-to-God East Ender who was something of a fairy godfather to the aged and infirm and the unlucky of the boxing game.

Thereafter the acquaintance had ripened into friendship, for Bert had discovered that the Toff had no particular dislike of smallpart crooks, knowing they were simple folk and honest according to their lights. Moreover, anything or anyone whom the Toff saw at Bert's was safe from the police as far as he was concerned.

And then, one day when the Toff had been in need, Bert had sent two or three of his clients on a punitive expedition at the Toff's behest, and thereafter they had a working arrangement.

Bert answered the telephone.

"Bert's gym," he said, and hiccoughed.

"I thought it might be," said the Toff, and instantly Bert said how glad he was to hear from Mr. Ar, how was he? why hadn't he been over lately, and what was he up to now?

"I'm not too sure about that last," said the Toff, "but I could find a job for two or three of the boys, Bert."

"Name yer men," said Bert simply.

"I'll leave that to you," said the Toff. "But get them off quickly, and have them watch Dring Mansions in Park Lane. There's a couple named Lorne living in Flat 81. A small red-haired woman and a big blond bloke not unlike a Swede to look at. I'd like to know where they go, and when."

"Leave it ter me," said Bert.

"Good man," said the Toff. "I'll call or phone in a day or two, but don't be surprised if I'm longer."

"You," said Bert, with something that sounded like a hoarse chuckle, "won't never surprise *me,* Mr. Ar. Nuthink you does ever surprises me." He chuckled again, and the Toff said goodbye, to turn and find Ted Harrison staring at him.

"I suppose I'll get used to you," the Toff said, "but whenever I'm at the telephone you give me the impression that you're staring in a mood of complete hero-worship. It's embarrassing."

"Hero-worship!" exclaimed Harrison. "I'll have you know that I think most of this is nonsense!"

"As you told Fay," said the Toff gently.

Harrison grinned, and went off at a tangent.

"I've packed a few things for you, and if we're going to catch that train we ought to hurry. I'll ask questions on the train."

"Thanks very much," said the Toff humbly.

After leaving a note on the table, lest his man Jolly should return first, they left the flat and went by taxi to Euston. Again the Toff went to considerable trouble to find whether they were being followed, but they reached the station without any indications that they were, and found their carriage with its two berths.

"Night trains are never cheerful," said the Toff, "and if you continue to scowl like that this will be a record bad journey. What's on your mind?"

Harrison continued to look worried.

"Draycott, of course. I can't make head or tail of the business, and I'm wondering if we'll find him up there."

"Oddly enough," said the Toff. "I'm wondering exactly the same thing."

Chapter Seven

Night Journey

When they were on the way, and before they had changed for the sleeping-berths, Harrison demanded to know why the Toff was interested in the tenants at Dring Mansions. The Toff told him a little, although he did not mention that he had seen the red-haired Myra at Grey Street.

"If I'd been you," Harrison said, "I'd have had the police on them like a shot."

"And confused the trails and probably given yourself a lot of trouble."

"I don't see it."

"Well, look for it," said the Toff dryly. "Lorne and Myra were interested in me, and presumably the reason for their interest was Fay's call earlier in the evening. Obviously, she'd been followed."

"All right, there's no need to be so clever about it. I'm not used to working these things out like you. But why should anyone follow Fay?"

"Because they wanted to know why she was interested in the flat at Grey Street, and whether she would discover the dead body."

"That seems to fit," acknowledged Harrison.

"Thanks," said the Toff sardonically. "However, we can safely say that Fay was followed, and that the Lornes wanted to know whom she had come to see. Consequently Myra put over her act, but she was startled when she learned who I was. That's the queerest thing yet. Why should anyone suspect that I would become interested?"

"I don't know," said Harrison. "Except that you do turn up at awkward moments, don't you?"

"It has been known," said the Toff, with considerable understatement. "But even that doesn't explain why anyone should suspect that I might be involved in this particular case. The other factor is that there's someone who can give the Lornes orders."

"I suppose that is implied."

"It's more than implied, it's shouted at us," said the Toff. "But I think Bert Ebbutt's boys will look after the Lornes. Our worry is Draycott, or, more correctly, Fay. How well do you know her?"

"We've been friends for years."

"Good friends?"

"As good as I could make it. If I'd had my way, we would have been married a couple of years ago. But Fay always says 'No' in the nicest of ways. It wouldn't have been so bad," added Harrison quietly, "if there'd been someone else, but she just told me that she was never likely to feel more than—well, friendly. She had a tough time a year ago, and was six months without a job. She didn't tell me about it, but I discovered it by accident. I put her on to Draycott right away, and he fixed her up."

"Why didn't she tell you how things were?"

"It was my own fault, I suppose. She knew that I would start the old 'marry-me-and-have-no-worries' tune, and she preferred not to risk it. Anyhow, that's nothing to do with the case in hand."

"Except one angle," said the Toff.

"I'd rather not discuss it," said Harrison.

"It needn't take long. You've known Draycott for a long time, and you'll know whether he's the type to appeal to Fay."

"Do we have to go into that?"

"I'd like to."

"Oh, all right," growled Harrison. "I don't know about the 'type' to appeal, but I gathered that Fay had fallen for him. I worried her for years, and she kept putting me off, but she meets a man, her employer who's engaged, and she loses her head. I met her a fortnight after she'd taken the job, and …" Harrison cleared his throat and looked out of the window, and the moon shining on pale fields. "Jokingly I asked her whether she would give it up and change her mind about me. She just said: 'Especially not now, Ted. I'm sorry.' And that," went on Harrison, with a harsh note in his voice, "gave me a bad time for a day or so. I knew Jimmy Draycott wasn't the man to let anyone down, and even if he did respond to Fay's feelings nothing could come of it. Not that I think he dreamed—dreams, I mean—of what she thinks."

Rollison said reflectively: "Well, it's an odd mix-up, and a month—she's been working for him for a month, hasn't she?"

"It might be five weeks."

"A month isn't likely really to secure her interest, and when he's married that will probably sort itself out. Provided," added the Toff, "that he's alive."

Harrison took out his pipe and began to fill it, while the Toff leaned back against the cushion and appeared to doze. He heard Harrison say abruptly: "Now you've dragged this out of me, how does it help?"

"I don't know yet," said the Toff. "It's a bad break, but you've had time to get used to it."

"Oh, it doesn't worry me much now," said Harrison.

But he was not convincing, and the Toff considered this new personal angle to the affair of Fay Gretton. He was not altogether surprised, but there was one thing which puzzled him.

Why had Harrison sent Fay to see him?

Harrison must have suspected that the trouble was serious or he would have offered to try to get into the flat himself. Possibly Harrison felt too keenly the situation which had arisen between Fay and Draycott. Fay's insistence on avoiding the police – a reasonable insistence as things had been – could easily have made Harrison think of the Toff.

Nevertheless, Harrison *had* a motive for murder.

The Toff considered that point and decided that the motive was very slim. Had Draycott and Fay been engaged, or had there been any possibility of Draycott breaking one engagement for another, that would have given Harrison's position a completely new significance. Of course, he had only Harrison's word that Draycott knew nothing of Fay's feelings, but he could not imagine Fay showing them.

In a tortuous fashion the Toff had arrived at two suspects, Harrison and Fay: and because he made an unfailing practice of keeping all the possibilities in mind, he did not entirely close the gate on them.

Before leaving the flat the Toff had slipped a small automatic into his pocket, for he did not propose to be taken unawares again. He had not told Harrison that he was carrying it, but he kept it at his side in the bunk, tying it to his wrist with a small strap to make sure that it did not fall.

The rumble of the train-wheels did not disturb him, nor did the piercing shriek of the whistle as the train went through many stations: but a movement at the door did.

He opened his eyes.

There was a small light burning in the middle of the carriage ceiling. On the opposite berth Harrison was lying on his back, with his mouth open and a faint snore coming from his lips. Without his glasses, and in that dim light, he looked older and a little careworn.

But the snoring had not awakened the Toff.

He was facing the door, a position he had taken up deliberately, and he watched it slide open, inch by inch. He saw a man's hand coming more clearly into view as the sliding door opened. Then he saw the man's head and shoulders, recognizing nothing and hardly seeing the face, for the man's trilby was pulled well down over his forehead, and the Toff was unable to move to get a better view.

One thing was certain: it was not Lorne.

This man was shorter, and smaller in every way. He moved with a furtive stealth and yet with such precision that it seemed clear that he had entered feloniously on more than one occasion. He stepped into the carriage as the door was wide enough to admit him, and looked first at Harrison and then away.

Through eyes that looked closed in sleep the Toff saw the man stare at him, and saw the thin lips tighten. He had a better view of the face then, and was not impressed. It was sallow and thin, and the lips were set tightly and showed very little shape. The nose was long, and pinched at the nostrils. The eyes and forehead were completely covered.

The Toff gripped his automatic.

He maintained an even breathing, and the intruder did not suspect that he was being watched. A moment later the Toff relaxed, for the man went to his clothes – on a hanger at the foot of his bunk – and began to run through the pockets. He looked in the wallet, putting aside the twenty-odd pounds in notes which the Toff had with him, but he was not looking only for money.

He did not appear to find what he wanted in the wallet.

Carefully he went through each pocket, examining what few papers he came across, and as the search continued his lips grew tighter, and once, under his breath, he swore. He finished at last, then moved stealthily towards the Toff's head.

He had stuffed the notes into his breast pocket, and kept his left hand there. The Toff, who knew the ways of many of the criminal type too well to take chances, suspected that he was holding a cosh inside his pocket.

The man's right hand slid under the Toff's pillow.

The Toff waited until it was well there, and then moved. He shot out his hand and gripped the intruder's left bicep. The man gasped with the sudden pain, tried to wrench his arm away, failed, and then pulled his right hand out and punched viciously at the Toff.

The Toff punched back.

His blow landed on the side of the man's face, going downwards, and it sent him staggering against Harrison's berth. Harrison woke up with a start, while the Toff changed his grip and caught the little crook's left arm at the elbow. He increased his pressure, and the man groaned.

Harrison gasped: "What the devil's all this?"

"Keep quiet," said the Toff, *sotto voce,* "and come down. You can look after this joker for a moment."

Harrison did not waste time. His awakening might have been abrupt, but he was alert and active enough when he slid from his berth, gripped the little crook's arm, and watched the Toff move a hand to the man's pocket. When the Toff withdrew it he was holding a black lead-weighted cosh, which could have caused a serious injury.

"Keep him there," said Rollison.

It was then that the little crook wrenched himself free from Harrison's grasp and made a leap at the window, which was open a few inches. He wrenched at the door-handle, while Harrison made a grab at him, getting in the Toff's way.

The door opened.

Harrison cried out, and the other went forward, gripping the side of the door and clearly trying to get down to the footplate. But he slipped, and the Toff saw him disappear into the void. A shriek rang out and died away, but did not lose its horror.

Chapter Eight

The Queen's Hotel

The Toff stretched an arm upwards and pulled at the alarm cord, the shriek ringing in his ears. Harrison was standing at the open door, gripping the sides and swaying with the motion of the train.

"Move back, old chap."

Slowly Harrison obeyed. His face was pale, and his lips were parted.

"There's whisky in my case," said Rollison.

As he spoke the train was slowing down, and doors were banging farther along the corridor. Lights were shining from carriage windows which a few minutes before had been in utter darkness. A guard came hurrying towards the Toff's compartment, calling: "Who pulled that cord, please? Who pulled the cord?"

The Toff waited for the man to reach him.

"I did," he said, to a portly man with a silky brown moustache decorated with breadcrumbs. The guard was hatless, and his bald head was shiny.

"Well, what—'Ere, what are you doin' with that *gun!*"

His voice went upwards, and carried far along the corridor. Voices and mutters of conversation ceased, except that a woman said clearly: "Someone's got a gun, George."

"All right, m'dear," said the unseen George. "That's all right, the guard will look after it."

Rollison spoke slowly, shaken by the sudden jump from the window.

"Nothing, as it happens. A man has jumped out of my door."

"Jumped!" exclaimed the guard, and the woman who had called out before repeated in her clear, carrying voice: "He says a man has jumped out of the door, George."

"All right, m'dear, I can hear," said George.

It was that which broke the tension that had been in the Toff's mind from the moment the little man had disappeared. He uttered silent thanks to the unseen George, while two more guards came up to the compartment, both carrying lanterns. The Toff unfastened the gun from his wrist and placed it on his bunk.

"I'll give you what information you want later," he said. "Where are we?"

"Just running into Crewe, sir." The guard appeared to be reconciled both to the gun and the Toff's manner, but he remained in the carriage while the others jumped down to the track and walked back along the line. The Toff sat on the edge of his berth, smoking, and a few passengers passed by and stared into the compartment. Harrison glowered at them, and it occurred to the Toff that if ever a man looked guilty – of what it did not matter – Ted Harrison did then. But he had recovered by the time a messenger came to say that the body had been found.

"So he's dead," Harrison said.

"We were travelling fast," said the Toff. "He didn't have a dog's chance. The one thing that poor devil knew was that he must not be caught. He preferred to risk that jump."

"Isn't it time you told us about it?" asked the guard.

"They'll want me for an inquiry at Crewe, I take it?" said the Toff. "I'll get dressed."

He hoped that there would not be a long delay, and his hopes were vindicated. The assistant station-master on duty was satisfied with a brief outline of the story plus Rollison's name and address. That was helped by the willingness with which he offered to contact with Scotland Yard. In different circumstances he would have been amused by the officials, who gave the impression that they welcomed the tragedy because of the opportunity to meet him.

The Toff disliked the tragedy intensely.

It was not the death of a man that worried him. As with the man he imagined to be Draycott, the fact of death itself had no effect on him. But the desperation in the crook's mind had sinister implications.

Why had he been so afraid of being caught?

For the crime on the train he would have suffered no more than three years' imprisonment, and probably a lesser sentence: yet he had acted like a man who had committed murder and arrest seemed imminent.

Or a man who was afraid of other things.

"What other things?" asked Harrison. Both had dressed, and there was no thought of sleep. The train was moving at speed again.

"I don't know," said the Toff slowly, "but our man was possessed by the fear of the devil, and that is not a nice thing."

"You're a queer fellow, aren't you?" remarked Harrison.

The Toff shrugged but did not answer. He was still wondering about the dead man – on whom there had been nothing likely to help identification – when they reached Manchester. It was a fine, bright morning, with the sun just breaking over the horizon, and lending to the Lancashire city a touch of early-morning grandeur. The station was not busy, taxis were available, and the Toff and Harrison went at once to the Queen's Hotel.

The night porter was heavy-eyed and inclined to be surly. He did not know if there was a Mr. Draycott there, and if he did no one was going to be disturbed by him at six o'clock in the morning without orders. There was no chance of him calling the manager, either: what did he want – the sack?

A ten-shilling note made no impression. The porter was a north-countryman of the rare type who seemed to have a perpetual grievance. He was going to do nothing, although somewhat grudgingly he said that they could wait in the lounge.

"All right," said Rollison. "Go and make us some tea, will you?"

"Ah don't mind doin' that," said the porter. Harrison waited until he was out of earshot, and then snapped: "I wouldn't have handled him like that."

"If a bribe won't do it, shouting certainly won't, but our porter is a fool in his way. Come on." The Toff left the lounge, and, with Harrison on his heels, reached the reception desk. The Toff went to the clerk's side of the counter and lifted the heavy register.

"We know he's here, don't we?" Harrison said.

For the first time that morning the Toff showed signs of irascibility.

"Don't be a fool! I'd rather deal with a dozen porters than you."

Harrison stumped off towards the lounge. Rollison ran his forefinger down the list of entries. 'Draycott' was there – he had arrived two mornings before, on the morning when Fay Gretton had first missed him. He was in Room 45.

Rollison replaced the register and reached the lounge ahead of the porter, who brought both tea and biscuits. Rollison paid and tipped him. Harrison apologised and started to pour out tea. Rollison watched the porter straightening some tables, and they had nearly finished a cup of tea when the man went out.

Rollison replaced his cup promptly.

"We're going upstairs," he said. "We'll use the staircase, and with luck dodge the porter or anyone else who might be about."

Harrison drew a deep breath.

"You're going up, of course, and you got his room number from the book. I'm too tired to have any sense, Rolly. Kick me next time I get obstreperous!"

"It wouldn't surprise me if I took you at your word," said the Toff.

They were seen only by a maid as they hurried up, to find a small plaque on the second-landing wall pointing to the room numbers 32 to 50.

The Toff glanced at the door-locks as he went by, and was pleased yet not surprised to find they were of the old-fashioned kind. His pick-lock would make short work of the one on Draycott's door.

Room 45 was the last one on the right-hand side of the corridor, and an open window was admitting a chilly breeze as they reached it. There were no boots or shoes outside, although there were at most of the other doorways. Rollison would not be particularly surprised to find Draycott – or the man who was calling himself Draycott – had left.

Harrison watched him manipulate the key, and was grinning as the lock clicked back. Rollison took a quick glance along the passage, saw no one, and opened the door.

He stepped through with Harrison on his heels.

And he stopped abruptly, for he saw a man standing opposite the door covering him with an automatic. It was the second time that he had seen a gun in the hand of the man named Lorne.

Chapter Nine

Mr. Lucius Lorne

There was a moment of utter silence.

Earlier that morning the Toff had assured himself that he had been taken by surprise for the first and last time in this affair, but he was wrong, and admitted it. He would have said that the one thing he considered quite certain was that Lorne would not be in Manchester. But there he was, standing and looking as if he had had a full night's sleep, full of confidence, which was only partly explained by the gun in his hand.

"Come in, come in," said Lorne, and his voice was deep and mellow, not unlike it had been when the Toff had heard him for the first time chiding the redhead Myra. "I half-expected you, Rollison."

Harrison said in a hoarse whisper: *"I'll make a dash for it."*

Since the Toff was first in the line of fire, that was a sensible if risky suggestion, but Harrison was wrong, for as he spoke another voice came from behind him.

"Don't you believe it."

The Toff did not take his eyes from Lorne's, but he heard the second voice, and the thump which followed it. He assumed that Harrison had been struck with a cosh. He had walked into as carefully prepared a trap as he was likely to encounter, but even then the most surprising thing was the speed with which it had all been arranged. He was less afraid than puzzled, because it seemed as if Lorne had expected him here.

Lorne must have flown from London.

The Toff went forward a pace as Harrison was lowered to the floor and dragged into the room. Then the door was closed by a chunky, broad-shouldered man dressed in an ill-fitting blue suit.

"I'm sure you won't make the same mistake as your friend, Rollison," said Lorne almost jovially. "Quite an unexpected meeting, isn't it?"

"Up to a point, yes."

"And such a pity that you did not herald your call with one of those interesting little cards," added Lucius Lorne. "You are a peculiar man, Rollison, with quite a reputation, and yet interested in such puerilities."

The Toff, who was some twelve inches from the wall, went back and leaned against it. He looked a little tired, and his eyes were half-covered by lids that dropped more than he often allowed them, but his poise was a thing to marvel at. His manner gave no idea that there was an armed thug at his side – Harrison was on the floor and still unconscious – and another man in front of him, while he regarded Lorne with no more than polite curiosity.

In fact, the Toff looked bored.

"'Puerilities'," he said reflectively. "Quite a big word for you, isn't it? Or did Myra tell you about it when she jumped at seeing the card?"

Lorne's eyes lost their humour.

"Keep that mouth of yours shut."

"And now we sink to a lower stratum," murmured the Toff. "I hardly expected you to keep it up for long. But about those cards of mine. It's always interesting to get the other man's point of view, and if they could be improved—"

"Guv'nor, do we *'ave* to listen to this?"

The Toff regarded the man with a fresh interest. The accent was Cockney, which was hardly surprising, for it was not to be expected that Lorne would have natives of Manchester to help him. A short, broad-shouldered, coarse-faced man, with a scar from an old burn under his right eye which did not improve his looks. His eyes were brown and small.

"Please yourself," answered the Toff, "but if you don't want to listen, go away." He smiled at Lorne. "Don't you get tired, holding that gun?"

Lorne's lips tightened.

The Toff was satisfied with one thing: he had Lorne guessing, and it was good when the other side was unsure. Lorne had expected him to crack when he was faced with the gun and the knowledge that he had been tricked, but it was not the Toff's habit to crack, although there were times when he pretended to. His chief interest was to undermine Lorne's confidence, and he was succeeding, for as Lorne grew angry so his confidence ebbed.

"Rollison," Lorne's voice grew high-pitched, "I warned you last night, and you took no notice. I can't afford to have you around."

"Oh, I don't charge much," said the Toff.

It was then that the little thug hit him.

The punch was delivered with force towards the small of the Toff's back, and landed heavily. But the Toff had seen it start, and held himself slack. The blow hurt, but not excessively, and as it landed he turned, ignoring Lorne and the gun, and took a chance which he knew might prove fatal.

His right fist went like a piledriver for the man's chin, taking him so much by surprise that he watched the blow coming but did not dodge. It struck him with a *crack*! that echoed through the room, lifted him from his feet and landed him on the floor two yards away. His eyes rolled, and he did not move.

The Toff said: "I don't want to lose my temper, Lorne, but your roughnecks aren't helpful. Don't imagine that gun will help you. The place will be raided at the first sound of a shot."

Lorne snapped: "This silencer will drown it. You can't bluff me."

"No?" said the Toff inquiringly. "My dear fool, you don't imagine that I came here unprepared? Or that I thought there was any chance of the real Draycott being here?"

"I don't care what you thought!"

"It's always a mistake to underrate your opponent," said the Toff, and then – as throughout that strange interview – it was as if he had the gun and the upper hand, and was able to dictate the conversation.

He slid one hand into his pocket, and Lorne raised the gun two inches.

"Oh, don't act like a school-kid!" said the Toff testily. "I'm here, and others will be soon. If you want a cut-and-dried case for murder against you, shoot and be damned. If you'd rather have a chance to avoid the Draycott charge, get out."

Lorne said: "You're lying. And I didn't kill Draycott."

"Really?" The Toff brought out his cigarette-case and his lighter, lit a cigarette and tossed the case gently towards Lorne. "Smoke?" he added.

It was the simplest of things.

The case curved an arc through the air, and was aimed to land about the region of Lorne's waistband. Lorne either had to dodge or to make an attempt to catch it. He tried the latter, and for a moment the gun was pointing away from the Toff. Rollison moved his right hand to his trousers pocket and his own gun. He fired through his pocket. His bullet went wide, but the report was loud, and enough to make Lorne jump and then go pale.

"Want another?" demanded the Toff, and his voice was very hard. "One to warn, and the other to mean business. We'll shoot it out if you like." Lorne said in a strangled voice: "Remember what I said about making a charge. If anyone comes, send them away!"

The echo of the shot had faded, but there were footsteps outside. The Toff knew that Lorne was as desperate as ever he would be, and that if the door opened he would try to shoot his way out. There was no point in risking that: and for the moment the Toff preferred Lorne at large than in a police-station cell, although undoubtedly Chief Inspector McNab would have said that he was wrong. A sharp knock came on the door. The Toff said: "It's all right, thanks."

"Ah heard shooting," called a North-country voice. "Ah swear it coom from here, sir."

"It's nothing to worry about," said the Toff. "I'll see you in ten minutes if you care to come back." He did not seem to think it possible that whoever was outside would insist on coming in, and after a pause footsteps retreated from the door. Lorne was breathing hard, and his forehead was beaded with sweat. Quite slowly the Toff took his gun from his pocket, for Lorne had been intent on watching and covering the door. "Put that gun down," Rollison ordered. Lorne took one look at him and obeyed. Harrison made a peculiar gasping noise, and sat straight up as if operated by a switch. He stared uncomprehendingly at the Toff and Lorne. "I'd rinse my face if I were you," said the Toff easily. "Things have changed, and Lorne is now going to tell me a pretty story."

"I'm saying nothing!" cried Lorne.

"You have a peculiar habit of talking in exclamation marks," said the Toff. "However, I'm not going to waste a lot of time. You flew here, didn't you?"

"Supposing I did?"

"Who told you I was on my way?"

Lorne said, with a slight return of his earlier confidence: "I had you watched, but you didn't realise it. You were followed to Euston, and I guessed where you'd be making for."

"That's fine," the Toff said. "So you arranged for the fake Draycott to telephone Harrison from here, did you?"

Lorne swore: "Why, you swine—!"

"There you go into the purple again," said the Toff, "and you still don't impress. I wonder why you wanted to create the impression that Draycott was still alive? Perhaps you hoped that the body wouldn't be discovered yet, and a call to the flat would have made it inevitable. You arranged for the call from here, but not until after Miss Gretton and I had looked in at Chelsea. Right?"

"Supposing it is?"

It was right, of course.

Harrison bathed his head and face, dried himself on a soiled towel, and looked at the Toff with amazement.

"How did you do this?"

"Chiefly by persuasion," said the Toff. "Lorne is a beginner, and beginners are always easy. We now know that Lorne was most anxious that Draycott's body should not be found so soon. Too bad, wasn't it? And of course," he went on musingly, "he followed—or preceded—us up here because he was afraid I knew enough to put him inside for the murder. A very proper fear too," added the Toff.

"But what I said at Dring Mansions still holds good, Lorne. I want the bunch of you."

"You'll never get us." Lorne was very pale.

"So there *is* a gang!" exclaimed Harrison.

"And now you're getting the exclamation-mark complex," said the Toff. He put his head on one side and regarded Lorne thoughtfully. "I can't make up my mind what to do with you. You can't stay at liberty, and you certainly can't stay here. I think perhaps you'll talk more easily to me than to the police. I—"

There was no tap on the door, but it opened abruptly, and he saw two men. They looked as if they knew which end of a boxing-glove should be used for the greatest effect. They were hefty and husky, and the first of them said: "Put that gun down, you!"

The Toff did not obey; but neither did be use the gun, for a missile that he did not at first recognise came through the air from the second newcomer and struck his arm. The gun dropped, and then Lorne turned.

Towards the windows!

It was open at the bottom, and he pushed it up swiftly and climbed through. The Toff could do nothing, and when Harrison made a rush one of the newcomers caught his arm. Lorne scrambled outside, and from the fact that he stood upright the Toff guessed there was a fire-escape. The clanging of his footsteps proved it.

It happened so quickly that it was hard to believe it was true, but the missile – a stone, as it turned out – had caught his funny-bone; and a simple thing like that could easily incapacitate him.

"And that takes care of Lorne for the time being." He regarded the two huskies calmly but without approval. He did not think that either man was armed, or the guns would have been shown by then. "Who are you?"

The first man, taller, blunt-faced, and with a truly remarkable cauliflower ear, said slowly: "Was that Mr. *Rollison*'!"

"Oh, my God!" exclaimed Harrison. "What is this?" And the Toff, very softly, laughed.

"It's a joke," he said. "And if you can see it that way it's funny. No, George. I'm Rollison." The husky roared: *"What's that!"*

"I'm Rollison," said the Toff, and went on: "and you, of course, are friends of Bert?"

"That we are that," said the speaker, and his villainous face took on an expression of such abject self-reproach that even Harrison smiled. "Bert got on t'phoon and told us t'coom right here, after we'd seen a man come by t'airyplane from London. Meaning," he added confusedly, "we were t'follow t'man, that's so. We didn't see him, mister, but we found that he'd coom up here—"

"A case of mistaken identity, George."

"Ah'm Harry, if ye don't mind."

"Of course not, George," said the Toff. He talked for some thirty seconds, showing a real grasp of the essentials. He had wondered how Lorne had left London without the attentions of Bert Ebbutt's men; but it had not happened. Lorne had been followed to the airfield, and Bert had telephoned Manchester friends to watch for his arrival. A slight mishap, and then misapprehension – and Lorne was at large in Manchester. Harry and his companion were full of apologies.

"It fitted in with what I wanted," Rollison said, and meant it. "But if you want to try to help, get some friends—as many as you like—and have the airfield and the stations watched for the man who got away. Will you?"

"Ah will that!" said Harry dubbed George.

He went, with his companion, at the double; and the Toff went downstairs, paying Lorne's bill to prevent an inquiry. Lorne, it proved, had booked a room by telephone and had arrived in at three o'clock that morning, omitting to sign the register after booking the room under the name of Williams. But, what was more important to the Toff and Harrison, the maids and the waiters at the Queen's remembered 'Mr. Draycott' well. A tall, thin, dark-haired gentleman who had arrived late three nights before. On the previous night he had had dinner in his room again – he had taken all his meals there. And he had asked for his bill early that morning.

"But Draycott's fair-headed, Rollison," Harrison said. "It was someone else, and that means Draycott *is* dead." This when they were in Room 41, which the Toff was allowed to use after saying that he was proposing to wait for Draycott, but if the latter did not arrive he would pay the bill.

The Toff said sharply: "Draycott's what?"

"Fair-headed. Almost blond, in fact." And then the Toff said slowly: "He is, is he? Well, the poor beggar at the flat was as dark as I am, so Draycott probably isn't dead."

Chapter Ten

Talk Of Draycott

Harrison, sitting on the edge of the bed, stared at the Toff as if he could not believe his ears, and then said clearly that he had never come across such nonsense. Why hadn't the Toff said that the dead man was dark? Fay would have been saved a lot of anxiety.

"It didn't occur to me," said the Toff. "I'm sorry about Fay. However, it was *prima facie* evidence which failed us for once, but it makes the problem greater. Where is Draycott, if he's not dead and hasn't been here?"

"The Lord knows," said Harrison. "What are we going to do now?"

"We'll wait for George's report—or was it Harry?—and then we'll get back to London. I hope," added the Toff very slowly, "that we didn't make a mistake in letting the girls go off on their own. If I've been followed so freely, they might also have been."

Harrison stared with increasing anxiety.

"Rollison, Fay's not in danger, is she?"

"I hope not," said the Toff. "But I've committed a grave sin of omission. What time is it?"

"Half past seven."

"I'll call Anthea," said the Toff.

There was little delay on the call to Kensington, but Anthea did not answer. Jamie, her husband did. No, there had been nothing out of the ordinary at 1023 Bayswater Road, and the two girls were sharing a room. Was he quite sure? Hadn't he seen them when he had said good night to his Anthea?

"Oh, all right," he said when the Toff insisted that he look in the room again. "But I wish you wouldn't make such a fuss, Rolly."

He was away only for a few seconds, and then said: "Ay, they're both there and sleeping soundly. You don't want to disturb them, do you?"

"I do not," said the Toff. "But I do want you to tell Fay—if you've reached the stage of calling her Fay—that there's evidence that Draycott isn't dead."

Jamie Fraser promised that he would tell her the moment she awakened, and that he was very glad indeed. That earnest young Scotsman rang off, and the Toff put through another call to Bert's Gymnasium. He did not discuss the fiasco of that morning, but asked Bert to have two men watching the Bays-water Road house. Bert agreed with alacrity, and the Toff rang off.

They breakfasted well, and the Toff had his clothes valeted. By that time several of the men who had been looking for Lorne had reported – through the still apologetic Harry – that they had found no trace of him. By noon there was still no word, and the Toff could only assume that Lorne had left the city by car; it was unlikely that he would stay in Manchester – unless he wanted to contact with the man who had passed himself off as Draycott.

Rollison did not talk much on the way back to London, which they reached just after six o'clock. In the last ten minutes of the journey, by cab to Gresham Terrace, Harrison said with feeling: "Well, it looks to me as if you'd better get the police searching for Draycott, Rollison. Or get him found somehow."

"With Draycott alive, our old friend *prima facie* turns up again," said the Toff. "Draycott could have killed the man at the flat, and McNab will certainly think it likely."

"I suppose you're going to wait for something to turn up?"

"Plenty will, without my waiting for it. In fact I expect there'll be something on the doorstep when we get to Gresham Terrace," said Rollison.

There was a police constable, with a request that Mr. Rollison visit Scotland Yard at once, and would he please telephone Inspector McNab that he was on the way? The Toff said that he would, while Harrison decided to get back to his own flat.

The Toff reached Scotland Yard, and nodded and smiled at the many who recognised him there. He did not need to send his card in, for he had telephoned, and McNab had sounded impatient to see him. McNab shared an office with three other Chief Inspectors, but owing to holidays he was alone.

As tall as the Toff but for an inch, big and chunky, fair-haired although going grey, and with heavy features that could be – and often were – aggressively hostile, McNab was sitting at a desk with a pile of buff-coloured papers in front of him. The Toff saw him signing one of them as he opened the door, and then McNab looked up and pushed his chair back. His face cleared for a moment, and then he scowled. But he shook hands.

"Sit down, Rolleeson. I'm glad ye've got here. Where the de'il have ye been?"

"Right up to Manchester to stay at the Queen's," said the Toff.

"Ach, don't play the fule, mon," said McNab, and settled back in a swivel chair. "What have ye been doing?"

"Well, I'm not sure," said the Toff, "but supposing you tell me why you're so anxious to see me first?"

"I'll do that," said McNab, and pulled at his upper lip. "Why did ye lie to me about the body at Chelsea?"

"Did I lie?"

"Ye know damned well that ye did. Ye told me it was a body named Draycott, an' ye knew it wasn't."

"Omniscient though I would like to be," said the Toff, "I'm not. I knew Draycott lived there and there was a letter addressed to him in the pocket. I took too much for granted, but I acted in good faith, and lost no time in telling you about it."

"And let it be understood that ye must make a habit o' that, Rolleeson. However, I'm hopin' that ye know who the dead man is."

"I wish I did."

"Noo listen," said McNab earnestly; "don't keep things tae yereself, Rolleeson, that matter's too important for that. If ye knew the murdered man, tell me."

"I still don't," said the Toff. "Well, where's Draycott?" demanded McNab. The Toff smiled, knowing that was the main question which McNab wanted to put. McNab kept his features expressionless, save for his eyes; and those, blue and at times frosty, could not hide his disappointment as the Toff sadly shook his head.

"Mac, that wasn't worthy of you, but I don't know where he is. Oddly enough, I've been trying to find him, but he wasn't in Manchester."

"What made ye think he was?"

"I'll tell you," said the Toff.

There was little that he need keep to himself, except the fact that he might have sent for the police and given Lorne in charge. He told the rest of the story, including the remarkable affair of the man who had chosen to jump from an express train rather than be taken captive; and he was not surprised when McNab fastened on that as the most important angle.

"Draycott's playing some deep game," said McNab, who had a habit at times of talking as if police work was a continual international rugby scrum, and at others of talking in the most astonishing of understatements. "That will explain arranging for someone to impersonate him at Manchester. But for a man t'kill himself rather than be caught—it's verra bad, Rolleeson."

"For once," said the Toff, "we are agreed."

"I'd heard of the affair," said McNab. He had been advised by the Crewe police, and was sending Detective-Sergeant Wilson – who was usually his *aide* – to try to identify the body. But, "If we didna know him, Wilson isna likely to. Well, now, I've seen Draycott's fiancée and her family, an' they're reluctant to talk much. It wouldna surprise me," added McNab, "if they knew that Draycott was hiding from us."

The Toff said slowly: "It could be."

"It's shouting at us. Draycott killed the man at the flat, and was hoping it wouldna be discovered until he had an alibi. But something's gone wrong wi' his arrangements, an' he'll need a mighty good alibi to save him now."

"And I thought," said the Toff, "that an Englishman was always innocent until he was proved guilty. However, I wasn't referring to Draycott's part in this. I meant that the Harvey family could know something about it."

"What do ye know of them?" demanded McNab.

"Oddly enough, I haven't met them."

"If I believed all ye tell me, ye've seen no one in the case," said McNab sourly. "I wish I could believe ye more, Rolleeson, but ye tell such lies."

"At which I should be affronted," said the Toff. "Yet I'm not. Tell me more of the Harveys."

McNab had not a lot to say. Mr. Mortimer Harvey was a wealthy man, who had recently retired from – and yet still took an interest in – the Mid-Provincial Building Society. A prominent society, and while he had been director Harvey had received a salary of some ten thousand pounds a year. McNab, for some reason, was always interested in salaries when they reached what he privately considered unjustifiable proportions.

There was the daughter, Phyllis; a son, Gerald; and the wife, whom McNab dismissed as of no importance. The son was away from England.

The Toff heard the story, leaned back in his chair, and said reflectively:

"And you think the Harveys know something about Draycott's whereabouts?"

"It wouldna surprise me."

"I suppose Draycott met them in the way of business?"

"Ay, in a way. When Draycott worked for his uncle, Harvey was by way of being a friend of the family, and that's how they met. Graham Draycott—the uncle—was a much bigger agent than his nephew, until he went bankrupt. And thereafter it seems that Draycott had some difficulty in getting Harvey's approval of his courtship." McNab rolled the word 'courtship' round his tongue, as if to savour it fully.

"You haven't missed much, Mac. What are you doing about it?"

"I'm having the girl watched."

"In the hope that she'll lead you to Draycott?"

"There could be less likely things than that," said McNab aggressively. The Toff hastily agreed that many less likely things could happen.

"Don't you know the dead man?"

"Not yet."

"And you've found no motive?"

"I've had less than twenty-four hours," protested McNab. "I canna pairform mireecles, even if ye think ye can. All the same," added McNab more quietly, "the part the man Lorne is playing is peculiar. Would ye put him down as a man who's used to crime?"

"I would."

"And he appears to employ a number of men," said McNab. "It's a complication I didna want, Rolleeson. I was thinking it was a nice cut-and-dried murder with a personal motive. But it looks as if it might be bigger than that."

"Again we are agreed," said the Toff.

He left soon afterwards and walked back to Gresham Terrace.

It was the first time since he had admitted Fay to the flat that he had been left alone for more than a few minutes. He intended to spend at least an hour at Gresham Terrace, trying to grapple with the many problems, and particularly the many apparently disconnected angles of the affair. On the one hand it looked a self-contained crime: Draycott having murdered a man at his flat and now being intent only on escaping from the police. The Lorne angle widened it; the man who had jumped from the train made it yet wider, and the fact that to McNab it seemed that the Harveys were hiding something.

Rollison reached 55 Gresham Terrace and went upstairs slowly, his mind already working smoothly and the various factors appearing *en masse,* ready to be sorted out and as nearly as possible put in their right categories. But he was doomed to disappointment, for he found that Jolly had returned, and that there was a visitor.

She was in the small lounge, and: "She has been waiting for half an hour, sir, although I was compelled to advise her that I had no certain knowledge of the likely time of your return."

"Patience being a virtue, she's none the worse of that," said the Toff, and then, a little hesitantly: "It isn't Madam Litinov, Jolly?"

"In view of your freely expressed determination to have nothing more to do with the lady, sir, I should not have admitted her had she called." Jolly was dry and impersonal, and yet his eyes were smiling. "It is a Miss Harvey, sir."

The Toff stared.

"*Harvey?*" A pause. "Sure?"

"I did not have the temerity to ask for proof, sir, but that is the name on her card."

And the Toff took the card, which told him that Miss Phyllis Harvey lived at 9 Park Street, St. John's Wood, raised one eyebrow above the other in silent contemplation of Jolly.

"I'll see to her, Jolly. And by the way, does the name Draycott mean anything to you?"

"I cannot recall it, sir."

"I was afraid not," said the Toff. "All right, we'll do this in style. Announce me, and keep your ears open."

Chapter Eleven

Miss Phyllis Harvey

To say that the Toff was surprised was only partly true. He was at once surprised and pleased and puzzled. He had wanted to meet Draycott's fiancee, and had wondered how it could be contrived.

He had another surprise as he saw the girl.

Harrison had done her much less than justice. Nothing had prepared the Toff for so lovely a creature, and yet as he shook hands he wondered whether Harrison was not right after all; for Phyllis Harvey had a Madonna-like beauty of feature, with eyes large and blue and appealing, with soft lips barely touched with lipstick, cheeks a creamy pink and white which appeared to owe little to rouge, and dark hair drawn back severely from her broad forehead and set in plaits. A beautiful picture, and yet as expressionless as one drawn to scale and not by inspiration. Even when she spoke the Toff gained an impression that she was speaking carefully and deliberately although her voice was low-pitched and could be called 'sweet'. She was of medium height, and by no means thin. She wore a black 'cocktail gown'. She was hatless, and had a sable stole drooping back from her shoulders.

The Toff believed that she took drugs; the irises of her eyes were strangely minute, and her manner strengthened the suspicion.

"I do hope," she said, "that I am not disturbing any of your arrangements, Mr. Rollison?"

The Toff assured her that his arrangements were always flexible. She did not smile, but went on: "Thank you. You will, of course, guess why I am here?"

She was talking like a book, thought the Toff; a textbook and not one for an advanced class. He had a peculiar impression that she was speaking as if she had rehearsed a lesson and that every word needed a conscious effort of memory. She was the reverse of natural – and so the reverse of Fay Gretton.

"Is 'guess' the word?" asked the Toff. "It's about Mr. Draycott, I take it?"

"That is so." She was silent for a moment, and her lips quivered. Then: "I am so distressed, Mr. Rollison. I hardly know what to do, nor whom to consult. I was advised by a friend that you would most likely be able to help me."

"Who was it?"

"I—" She hesitated, as if the question had caught her unawares and she had not rehearsed an answer; if that was so she made an impromptu quickly and convincingly: "I hardly like to mention names, but it was a friend of my father's, a Mr. Seward."

"Ah!" said the Toff. He knew a Geoffrey Seward, and Seward lived in St. John's Wood. It was as likely a way of introduction as any, and he passed it by. "And what can I do?"

"I don't know," Phyllis Harvey said, and she began to talk swiftly, yet without feeling; from time to time she paused, and her lips quivered. The Toff wondered whether he had misjudged her earlier manner, and whether it was explained not by careful rehearsal, but by the fact that she was distraught.

She told him that her fiancé had left London unexpectedly, and without warning her, but that on the following day he had telephoned and told her that he might be kept from London for several weeks. Seeing that he was planning to be married within ten days, that startled the Toff. But, said Phyllis Harvey, James Draycott made it clear that the matter was one in which his personal safety was threatened. He had told her no more than that, but asked her to be patient. Only when she had insisted had he given her an address where she could contact him in emergency.

The Toff was sharply interested.

"And you have that address?"

"It is that which causes me so much distress," said Phyllis Harvey slowly. "After—after the visit from the police, and the tragic discovery at James's flat, I feel torn two ways. Justice demands that I advise the police where to find him, but my personal loyalty says otherwise. What *must* I do?"

"How far are you prepared to trust me?"

"That is a difficult question. I think that I could safely say that I am prepared to abide by your decision. If you think I should tell the police I will do so."

The Toff said sharply: "You think Draycott committed the murder, don't you?"

For a moment he wondered whether his sharpness would do more harm than good. The girl opened her mouth with a quick intake of breath, showing him for the first time that her teeth were as perfect as the rest of her features. Her eyes showed she was afraid, but it might be mental fear, anguish that her silence had forced on her.

"Why should you suggest that?"

"I didn't suggest it, I asked a question."

"It—it isn't wholly true," she said, and he breathed more easily when he saw that he had not closed her up. He imagined that she could be obstinate. More softly, he said: "I think it must be, Miss Harvey. Either you believe in him or you don't. What reason have you for thinking that he committed it?"

"I—I hardly know."

"Try to think," urged the Toff.

He was conscious then of a peculiar fact: he was out of patience with Phyllis Harvey, and it was not often he was out of patience with a beautiful woman. Her manner irritated him, although he tried to persuade himself that it was because he was tired.

"Well, I know that he has been—how *shall* I put it?—very worried at times. There has always been something which he has not discussed with me, and that made him seem" – she paused – "*afraid*.

And it was a week ago that he received a letter while I was with him, at his office. He said: 'I'll kill the swine before I've finished.'"

"And then!" asked the Toff, for she stopped.

"He laughed it off," said Phyllis Harvey. "He said it was a lot of nonsense. It was some trouble with a business transaction, in which I believe he had been bested."

"By whom?"

"I have no idea."

"It was a large one?"

"I inferred so."

"I see," said the Toff, and he stood up, his hand thrust deep in his trouser pocket. "Well, my advice is that you do not give the police the address for another forty-eight hours, Miss Harvey, but that you do tell me."

"I will do that," she said.

She had come prepared, for she took a card from her handbag, a silver chain affair, and handed it to him. The Toff glanced at the address, which ran:

ALLEN COTTAGE, HURLEY
HANTS.

"Thank you," said the Toff, and as she stood up he assured her that if it were possible he would find the precise truth before the police learned where to find Draycott. In the same mechanical manner with which she had started that peculiar interview she thanked him, and he showed her to the door, then hurried after her so that he could get her a taxi. She gave her father's St. John's Wood address. The Toff went back, to find that Jolly had prepared sandwiches and coffee. They talked while he ate.

"And so, Jolly, we come to the most peculiar fact of all."

"Through Miss Harvey, sir?"

"Yes. Haven't you seen it?"

"Not yet, sir," admitted Jolly. "If you will give me a moment or two for further consideration—"

"I'll tell you, and watch the effect with gratification." The Toff bit a sandwich, and went on: "She greeted me by saying that of course I guessed why she had come. But there was no reason why I should guess, as far as I was concerned. No one except Miss Gretton, Mr. Harrison, Bert—and we can count Bert out—and the police know that I was aware that Draycott was missing. So why should Phyllis think I should guess?"

Chapter Twelve

West End Spotlight

Jolly was a remarkable man.

The Toff had been able to give him only the briefest of *résumés*, and yet Jolly grasped the essentials, and was aghast at his failure to notice something so simple but of outstanding importance.

"I'm sorry, sir. The inference, of course, is obvious."

"Yes. Meaning that Phyllis Harvey knows more than she pretends. Well, that might be the case, but it might also be that someone has carefully primed her. She had all the appearance of being primed, and I'll agree with McNab that she was holding out on us. Allen Cottage, Hurley, Hampshire. You probably passed quite close to it when you went down yesterday."

"And when I returned today, sir. I remember the village—a most picturesque and charming place."

"Good. Go down there, and if Draycott is on the premises let me know at once."

"Very good, sir." Jolly hesitated. "You are sure that there is nothing I could do to greater advantage in London, sir?"

"Quite sure," said the Toff. "I shall look after myself, Jolly. Incidentally, the man Lorne is what might be called a beautiful blond beast, and as such you will recognise him. And the woman, Myra, is red-haired and with such amber eyes that you'll never mistake her."

"I will look out for them both."

"Good," said the Toff. "And now I'd better see how Miss Gretton is today."

Fay, it appeared, was in fine fettle, for since she had learned of the possibility that Draycott was alive she had thrown off the anxiety and was filled with *joie de vivre*. Anthea told the Toff of that, after Jolly had left for his second visit to Hampshire in two days. Anthea 'phoned, catching the Toff just before he left.

"She's downstairs with Jamie at the moment," said Anthea, keeping her voice low. "She's almost hysterical, Rolly. I didn't think a man could affect a girl like that."

"Your knowledge of men is small," murmured the Toff.

"Don't joke, please. Rolly …" Anthea's voice grew soft, and the Toff knew that she was about to make a suggestion that she expected him to oppose. "Have you been out lately?"

"I'm usually out," said the Toff.

"I mean by night. I mean," added Anthea desperately, "have you been to a night-club, or a cabaret, or—what I *really* mean," went on Anthea, speaking in a more normal and more pleasing voice, "is that I think it would do Fay good to have a night out. Only Jamie can't look after us both."

"My pet, I was awake for nine-tenths of last night."

"But you're used to that, aren't you?" said Anthea ingenuously. "A night without sleep now and again won't do *you* any harm. Or else you've disintegrated."

"Hush!" said the Toff. "That's the word my aunts like to use about me. Where have you decided to go?"

"You pet," said Anthea, and the Toff told her that he considered that she had lowered her technique considerably since she had married, and that if that was the way she wheedled Jamie she would have to mend her ways, for no Scotsman would stand for it for long. He also arranged to call for the party in two hours' time; that gave him precisely one hour and a half for sleep.

Nothing happened to disturb it.

He woke on time, dressed, and took a cab to 1023 Bayswater Road. He did not think that he was followed, although after his experience of the previous night, and the fact that Lorne – or someone working for Lorne – had successfully shadowed him while avoiding discovery, he was prepared to admit that it might have happened again.

Anthea had chosen the Can-Can Club.

It was off Shaftesbury Avenue, and, unlike most of its contemporaries, was housed in a large building, and the main part of the club was on the ground-floor level. The walls were of mirrors, the decorations in gilt and gold, and the floor – a large one for a night-club – was not of wood, but polished glass on wood. The food was fair, the orchestra – it did not say band – good, and the service excellent.

The Toff was not unknown there.

The manager, Frederick, bowed on seeing him, and insisted on showing them to the table which Jamie had reserved. The Toff brought up the rear, knowing that the party attracted considerable attention, for many eyes were turned towards them, and many women talked, while the men looked at Anthea and Fay and kept their thoughts to themselves.

Anthea was a vision in a gown of powder blue, and Fay in an evening-gown of black with white flowers at the corsage, and clearly, with her hair newly-dressed for the occasion, had that touch of the superb which made men gasp. The Toff, who was hardly unused to lovely women, was thoughtful when he considered the differences in Anthea, Fay and Phyllis. All three could justly be called beautiful, although Anthea only just scraped in.

He thought of Phyllis Harvey dancing here.

It was not likely to happen, and he shrugged the thought away Jamie, tall, broad, fair-headed, a Scotsman who could be dour and also charming, was in his most vivacious mood.

The orchestra played dreamily through *The Blue Danube,* as sleepily through *Rhapsody in Blue,* and then swung into *yeah, yeah, yeah.* Anthea and Jamie were dancing, and the other girl looked at Rollison seriously for the first time that night. She had not had too much champagne, but she had been keyed-up, and the Toff could understand what Anthea meant by saying that she was on the point of hysteria. Her good spirits, and vivacity, seemed unnatural.

Now she said: "Rolly, what does it all mean?"

He did not try to evade the issue.

"I don't know, but I hope to find out Fay, have you ever met a man named Lorne?"

"No."

"A woman named Myra?"

"No—what's she like?"

The Toff was about to explain when a waiter interrupted, a sleek and silent man who leaned over him and said softly: "Excuse me, sir."

"What is it?" asked the Toff, and then extended a hand to take an envelope which was being handed to him. "Who from?" he asked quickly.

"The gentleman arranged for it to be sent through several waiters, sir, in order not to be recognised."

"Oh." said the Toff, and made sure that he would recognise the waiter if he wanted to question him. The letter contained only a visiting-card, and on it – scrawled in block-lettering – the words:

RETURNED WITH THANKS – BE WISE,
AND DROP THIS BUSINESS.

The Toff stared down, and began to laugh.

It was a deep, rollicking laugh, and one that seemed to be of sheer enjoyment. It altered the expression on Fay's face, for she had been anxious when she had seen the note, and had followed his movements closely as he had opened it. It attracted people at nearby tables. It made the manager stare across the floor, and even started him towards the scene of this outrageous solecism, but he stopped when he saw who it was. It made the members of the orchestra peer in bewilderment, and it brought Jamie and Anthea from the floor. It did all that within two minutes, and it was two minutes before the Toff stopped laughing.

Then Fay said, very clearly: "If it's *so* funny, share it, please.'"

The Toff stopped himself from laughing again, and handed her the visiting-card.

"It's my own," he said. "I hoped to scare our Mr. Lorne with it. I'm beginning to appreciate that gentleman."

* * *

Jamie did not see that it was so very funny, and was inclined to resent the fact that attention had been drawn to the table. Anthea handled him, but Fay said quietly.

"I don't like it a bit."

"Don't you?" asked the Toff. They were dancing a slow foxtrot, and she was easy to dance with. "I've been sending out those cards for seven years; it's the first one returned, and I give our Luke full credit."

"Luke?"

"Myra called him Luke. Don't look so sombre, Fay. You're dancing with me, and you're in London's latest highspot. Your Jimmy is alive, and—"

"Please don't say that!"

The Toff said quickly: "I'm sorry, Fay. In some queer way I've been looking at Draycott as your private property, and it came out without warning. You fell pretty deeply in love, didn't you?"

She nodded. And she was close to tears, although he knew that there was small chance of breaking down. She had buoyed herself up with the belief that Draycott was not dead, but the stimulus would not last indefinitely. She went on quickly: "Rolly, what has he done?"

"Has he done anything?"

"Don't hedge, please. You know that he's in trouble of some kind. Rolly, he didn't kill that man did he?"

The Toff continued to dance with assurance. The orchestra was at its best, the gaily dressed and brightly lighted throng turned slowly and gracefully, while about them there was the hum of conversation, occasional laughter, the waiters threading their way amongst the tables. They were there, amid that crowd, and yet they were alone.

"I don't think so," said the Toff very quietly. "I don't know Draycott, but I've formed an impression of him, through you, Harrison and others. I feel it in my bones that he killed no one, but if you ask me to say why, I couldn't."

"Thank you for that," she said gratefully. "But the police are looking for him, aren't they?"

"I think so."

"Can you help him?"

"I hope so," said the Toff. "I think—"

But she did not hear what he thought, for he stopped speaking and stared across the big room, past a hundred people, towards a small party at a table in one corner. The table was secluded with palms and draperies, and yet from the corner of that dance-floor he could see all its members.

And Phyllis Harvey was there.

Chapter Thirteen

Action Again

Draycott's fiancée was there, and the Toff's card had been returned to him that night and in that place.

The two facts might be coincidental, but there was also a possibility that they were connected. He looked away from the party, but not for long, for Fay stiffened in his arms.

"Do you know her?" Her voice was a whisper.

"I've seen her," said the Toff, and he tightened his grip about her waist. "Chin up, Fay."

Fay said: "I've never seen her looking so beautiful. Oh, I hate her sometimes! I—" she stopped and forced a laugh. "Slap me, Rolly, or I shall get hysterics. Why do women have to be such cats about each other?"

It happened that the tempo of the dance quickened, and he swung her round more quickly, so that they were hidden from the party in the corner.

"How do you know cats hate? Fay, if you knew where Jimmy Draycott was, would you tell anyone you didn't know?"

Fay missed a step again, but recovered. The Toff saw the hope flooding her eyes.

"Rolly, do you know where he is?"

"I've been told where he might be."

"By—by Miss Harvey?"

"That is sheer guesswork, and I'll have nothing to do with it. You haven't answered the question."

"You know very well I wouldn't tell," said Fay, and then the music stopped and the Toff led her back to the table. Anthea and Jamie were watching them. Anthea was particularly pleased with life, and she said as they arrived: "Did you know that you make a nice-looking couple?"

"All of that is wasted," said the Toff. "What's more important is that the three of you are going to make a nice-looking trio, while I slip off for a word with Frederick."

The Can-Can's manager welcomed Rollison warmly. He was standing by the door, surveying the throng, and with justification he could have said that everyone seemed happy. Frederick, a Swiss was one of those men who liked to see a happy world, and was not primarily interested in money or profit, although he did not neglect them. He was short and he boasted considerable *embonpoint,* he wore the small, dark, waxed moustache which hotel and restaurant managers so often consider necessary. His brown eyes were gleaming as the Toff reached him.

"Ah, Mr. Roll'son, I was expecting to see you. Everyt'ing is perfeck, yes?"

"I couldn't ask for more," said the Toff amiably, "as far as service is concerned. But I am a worried man."

"M'sieul You a worried man! Oh no, no no, no! I, Frederick, cannot believe it." He beamed.

"I hope you'll try," said the Toff. He explained the matter of the note, and pointed out the sleek waiter who had handed it to him. Frederick frowned, scowled, clicked his teeth, and sent for the waiter. Thereafter it seemed to the Toff that a regular stream of sleek suave men came to Frederick, were questioned, and went away. It was the seventh man to be questioned who had been given the letter; when he had entered the foyer, by a man not in evening dress and who appeared to have arrived only a few seconds before. He had mentioned Rollison by name, explained that it was a joke and that he wanted as many waiters as possible to handle the letter.

The man had been tall, and very fair.

The Toff tipped the waiter and thanked Frederick, and returned to his table. He did not know whether to be pleased or disappointed that the card had not come from the table where Phyllis Harvey was sitting. Lorne had come in, and, what was worse, Lorne had followed him or had him followed.

The Toff disliked the thought that he could be trailed without noticing it. He did not get much opportunity to see the corner party, although in one dance he and Fay saw them clearly, and she told him that the grey-haired, austere-looking man talking to Phyllis was Mortimer Harvey.

A grey-haired, majestic-looking woman was not Harvey's wife but his sister. The other man of the party was neither old nor young, nor particularly prepossessing, although in a swarthy way he was handsome. He had a thin dark line of moustache, bold dark eyes, shining, wavy black hair. "That's Harvey's secretary, Mr. Ramsey," Fay said. "You seem to know the family well," said the Toff.

"Jim—Mr. Draycott does some business for Harvey, and Ramsey has been several times to the office. And I had to call at the house one evening with some papers. I saw them all then, and next morning he told me who they were."

"I see," said the Toff.

He was worried by Phyllis Harvey's presence at the club, for he did not think she was in a mood for gaiety and music. She still gave the impression of being somewhere else; still looked picture-beautiful and did not once dance, although her aunt danced, both with Ramsey, and Harvey. His impression that the girl was under the influence of drugs was strengthened.

"Did you meet Mrs. Harvey?" Rollison asked.

"No, she wasn't there," Fay answered. "They don't get on too well."

Rollison laughed. "I can imagine Harvey is difficult to live with. However, there's just no reason in the world why they shouldn't be here. Fay, do you feel like a breath of fresh air?"

"I'd love it," she said.

He took her to the foyer, and then into the street. A bright moon showed the people walking past, the occasional private car and taxi, and also a man who was standing on the opposite side of the road and looking very bored. A largish man, with a bowler hat.

"Well," said Fay, "have you seen what you wanted?"

"You don't miss much," said the Toff. "Yes, I've seen what I wanted, and I could be amused."

He did not enlarge on that cryptic statement, for he saw no reason why Fay should know that McNab was watching Phyllis Harvey. When they returned to Bayswater Road he told her that he had sent Jolly to investigate the possibility that Draycott was in hiding in Hampshire.

"I have a feeling that he is hiding from something that scares him, not the police. I think there's danger, and that he knows it, and is handling it the only way he thinks he can. Need I say more?"

"No," said Fay.

"Did you ever get any impression that he was scared or worried? At the office, or out of it?"

"No, none at all."

The Toff recalled Phyllis Harvey's assurance that Draycott had received a letter, and had threatened to 'kill the swine'.

"Has he been bested in any kind of deal lately?"

Fay looked startled.

"How did you know that?"

The Toff stood back from her, and sat on the edge of a chair, took out his cigarette-case and eyed her thoughtfully as he flicked flame to his lighter.

"I saw it as a possibility. You should have told me before if there was anything out of the ordinary happening in the past month. Don't *you* hold out on me."

"Oh, Rolly, please don't say that!" She was surprisingly young and naïve. "I didn't think there could be any connection. He had the agency for the Mid-Provincial Building Society, and he lost it. I think it was because he lost Mr. Harvey's support when Harvey resigned. It made a difference of a thousand a year to him, and I know he was worried by that. But when you said 'worried' I didn't think you meant in the way of business."

"I meant in any way. Who took the agency from him?"

"A firm in the West End—Murray and Firth. But that could not have any bearing, could it?"

"I don't know," said the Toff, "but I might find out. Well, it's time for bed." He had refused an invitation to stay at Bayswater Road, for he preferred to be at his flat during the night, and to commence operations from there the next morning. Jamie insisted on a nightcap, and the women left them together. Jamie measured the whisky, and said: "What do you think of this fellow Harrison?"

"Probably quite harmless."

"Oh yes. But hardly Fay's kind, d'you think?"

"Fay seems to agree," said the Toff dryly. "He came round earlier in the evening, didn't he?"

"Yes. He rather annoyed me," said the worthy Jamie. "He seemed to think that he was the only man for women—you know what I mean—who had any right to look after Fay. He rather got under my skin. However, it's of no account," added Jamie. "Here's to a quick solution, Rolly."

The Toff duly drank to the toast.

At home, he locked the door, put an automatic by his bed for the sake of security, and prepared for bed. It was nearly half past eight when he woke, and the night had been a quiet one. He lazed between the sheets for some minutes, yawned, went into the kitchen and put on a kettle, bathed and then made tea. He did not feel like cooking a breakfast, but made some toast.

At nine-fifteen the telephone rang, and he heard McNab say: "Rolleeson, why did Miss Harvey call to see ye?"

"I'm still trying to find out," said the Toff. "I think she was scared that you were taking things for granted against Draycott, and she came to make sure that I would stop it. Odd ideas some people have about me."

"Is that all the truth?" demanded McNab.

"I don't mind dealing with your scepticism in the evening, but first thing in the morning it's beyond me. She told me nothing I didn't know, and that you don't know. Next, please."

He heard a sound from the other end of the wire which might have been a laugh or a grunt. But there was nothing else McNab wanted to know, and he rang off. The Toff replaced the receiver thoughtfully, then took his Frazer-Nash from the garage near by and drove to Dring Mansions. There was no reply when he knocked and rang at the door of No. 81.

A clock from one of the flats was striking ten when he went to the end of the passage, and saw that a fire-escape led close to one of the windows of the Lornes' flat. He could not break in by the front door, but the window in question was open.

The back of the flats faced smaller houses, and he saw a few tradesfolk in the streets as he walked along the fire-escape without batting an eye, and saw then that by stretching up on tip-toe he could reach the window, He opened it more widely, and then climbed through.

He did not know whether he was observed, but hoped that the openness of what he was doing would allay any suspicion. He squeezed through the window and dropped lightly on the other side, finding himself in a small kitchenette, which was beautifully kept. He walked through to the front door, listening intently but hearing no sound in the passage. He waited there for some minutes, satisfied himself that no undue interest had been aroused, and then – all the time moving very softly and making no sound – he approached the doors of the two rooms which he took to be the bedrooms.

Neither was locked.

He turned the handle of one very quietly, but found a small bedroom empty, one which had not been slept in – unless the Lornes had been up early, and the flat had been straightened before they had left. He did not think that likely, and he approached the second bedroom with even greater caution. The door opened without a sound.

The bed had not only been slept in, but was still occupied. A man was sleeping, with the clothes dishevelled, and an eiderdown mostly on the floor. In sleep the man's homely features were relaxed, yet there was a frown at the lips, as if he were complaining in his dreams.

The Toff stared at Mr. Edward Harrison.

Chapter Fourteen

More Of Myra

The Toff stood quite still for some seconds, and recovering from the surprise at seeing Harrison there. It was no more than that, for he had had considerable doubts about Ted Harrison.

The Toff looked down at the key, inside the door.

He withdrew it, watching the sleeping man all the time, and closed the door quietly. He turned the key in the lock, perched his head on one side and looked at the door as if trying still to see Harrison, then he paid attention to the other bedroom. There was a small wall-safe behind a picture in the lounge. The safe presented little difficulty to the Toff, who was experienced in the ways of most locks. It contained only one thing of surprising interest.

There was a bundle of shares, some three thousand in all; and a covering letter fastened to them by a rubber band expressed Messrs. Murray and Firth's gratification that they had been able to obtain the shares for Mr. Lorne.

And the shares were in the Mid-Provincial Building Society.

* * *

By then the Toff admitted to himself that he was becoming exasperated with the Draycott affair.

So many trails started, only to end nowhere. Too many things happened behind his back: too many complications presented new problems, so that they continually increased and none showed any signs of approaching a solution.

Except for the Lornes there was no one he could try to interview, no one from whom information might be forthcoming – except Harrison. He decided that it would be wiser to let Harrison believe that the Toff thought his interest was a chivalrous one on Fay's behalf; Harrison would later get a shock.

He completed his search, and returned to the door of the main bedroom: Harrison was still sleeping, for only the sound of his heavy breathing came from the room. The Toff satisfied himself of that, put the key on the lounge table, then started for the front door. When he was two yards away he heard footsteps, and then he heard a key in the lock.

He moved swiftly towards the bathroom.

The door was open, and he slipped through, and then he found that by looking into a mirror above the hand-basin he could see the front door and most of the lounge. He kept one hand in his pocket about his gun and watched.

Lorne came in.

Behind him came Myra.

The door banged, and Lorne took off his hat and dropped it into a chair. He looked red-eyed and tired. The woman also took off her hat and patted her hair into position. He judged that she had been wearing the hat for some time, for her hair was very tight against her head.

"Thank God that night's over," Lorne said, and he stepped to a cabinet and helped himself to a whisky-and-soda, a bad way to start the day, and one that suggested he was not in a good state of nerves.

"It won't be long now, will it?" asked Myra.

"It would be over by now if we could find Draycott," said Lorne, and the Toff's heart jumped. "I'll slit Benny's throat when I see him again. He swore he'd got Draycott at the flat."

"Luke, don't talk like that!" There was courage in Myra, thought the Toff, and also something suggesting that she was not in crime for its own sake. "It's been dreadful, but there's no need to get so hardened to murder."

"Hardened?" Lorne sneered. "I'm hardened to it all right. I'm damned if I can understand why I'm on edge. There's no way it can be traced back to me. But I wish Benny would turn up," he added, and he drank his whisky. "That little runt will take himself into trouble one of these days."

"Luke—" Myra started, stopped, and then went on again breathlessly. "Luke, can't we get away from all this when it's finished? Do you have to associate with men like Benny and—and the others?"

The Toff saw the reflection of the man's face in the mirror. Lorne's eyes narrowed, and he stepped towards the woman.

"Now listen to me, Myra. There's one thing you've got to get into your head. This is the way I live."

"But, Luke—"

"There aren't any buts. I told you when we started that I didn't believe in working for a living, and I made a good one by being clever. Well, that stands. I can go about London as much as I like, and the police won't have a thing against me."

"But what about Rollison?"

Lorne swore. The woman flinched, and her face lost colour.

"All Rollison can do is talk; he knows nothing. I can handle fools of his type; I've been doing it since I was born. And if you don't like it you can clear out. Understand that."

"Oh, my God!" she said, and there was all the pain in the world in her voice.

"That won't help you," growled Lorne. "I'm tired of you moaning and complaining. You'd better get back to where you belong; it's nice and comfortable, and there's no danger. So, make up your mind."

The Toff's feeling was of pity for the woman, but contempt for Lorne. He could see her face, and knew that she was very close to tears. Lorne was glaring at her with flushed face and glittering eyes. His lips were wet and red, and he looked ugly.

"You—you don't mean that, Luke; you're tired." The voice desperate and afraid.

"I mean it all right. I've been working myself up to saying it for days. I can stand you when you keep your wits about you, but the way you missed getting Rollison to talk—"

"I—I hated that!"

"You hate everything. You'd make me go to church if you had your way. Well, listen to me." He stepped forward and gripped the woman's shoulder, and the Toff saw her flinch. "Listen—to—me," he repeated viciously. "You've linked up with me. You can stay and do what you're told, or clear out—I don't give a damn either way. But, whichever it is, you'll watch your step, and you won't talk. I can get you put behind bars, and it wouldn't worry me to see you there."

"Luke, don't say it! I thought—"

"You *thought*" sneered Lorne. "You're not the first I've strung along with and you won't be the last. A woman's no use to me if she ain't got guts" – the 'ain't' made the man seem even more brutal – "and doesn't know her place. Get that clear, you red-haired bitch."

The Toff saw her fists clench, and her eyes narrow. Suddenly she struck at Lorne on the right cheek. He was taken so much by surprise that he staggered. Then he jumped at the woman. She half screamed, but the sound was stifled in her throat, for Lorne's hand gripped it. Lorne was still swearing, acting like a man who had gone mad.

"I'll kill you—I'll squeeze the life out of you! I'll teach you to hit me, you whore!"

The Toff moved quickly, and reached Lorne without being noticed. He gripped the back of the man's neck with such pressure that Lorne gasped. Then he brought his knee up against Lorne's rear, jolted the man's spinal column and forcing him to release his grip. Myra fell. By then there was a sound from the bedroom, and the rattle of the door-handle. As the door failed to open, Harrison shouted: "What's the matter out there? Open this damned door!"

Lorne was trying without success to turn his head to see his attacker. The Toff increased his pressure, moving his fingers a little and getting round to the jugular vein. With Lorne gasping for breath, gasps which were getting fainter with each second, the woman making queer little moaning sounds, and Harrison shouting, there was bedlam.

Harrison stopped abruptly, as if he realised that if he brought strangers up it would cause trouble. The Toff did not relax his grip, but increased it, until Lorne suddenly went limp. He made sure that the man was not feigning.

The Toff bent down and ran through his pockets, taking out the wallet and all the papers. Next he took one of his own cards from his vest-pocket, one that had already been decorated with the little drawings of the top hat, the monocle and the swagger-cane. He scribbled across it:

Don't bother to return it.

Then he folded it and threaded it in one of Lorne's buttonholes.

Harrison was making an attempt to pick the lock.

The Toff took the whisky from the cabinet and moistened Myra's lips with it. A trickle that went into her mouth made her gasp and open her eyes. He did not know whether she recognised him or not, but he lifted her, and she stood swaying in front of him. The marks of Lorne's fingers were still red and ugly on her throat.

"You're coming with me," the Toff said, so quietly that he was sure that Harrison could not recognise his voice. The woman raised no protest, and he judged that with assistance she would be able to get downstairs. He opened the front door, closed it after helping her through, and then started the laborious journey to the lift. It was self-operated, and there was no one in the passage or in the hall when he reached it.

A taxi had just deposited a fare, and the Toff called him. He helped Myra inside, told the cabby to drive to 55 Gresham Terrace, and then he sat back and wiped the beads of perspiration from his forehead.

Myra sat in a corner, staring at him; he could not be sure whether her expression showed fear of him or whether it was the reflection of the horror she had experienced. That had been something she was not likely to forget.

She was steadier on her feet when they reached the flat, and the Toff sat her in a chair, kept the door of the kitchen open so that he could see her, and brewed tea. She looked woebegone and dreary even when she had finished it. The finger-and-thumb bruises on her throat were turning blue.

"Well," he said at last, "that was nasty. Do you feel that you can talk?"

She stared at him, and her amber eyes showed a sudden searing alarm. Her lips started to tremble, and she said in tones it was difficult to hear: "Why didn't you let him kill me? Why didn't you? I don't want to live, I tell you, I don't want to live!"

"It might not prove so bad," said the Toff.

But she went on sobbing, repeating wildly that she did not want to live. He left her in the room alone for a while, leaving the bedroom door open so that he could hear her.

He thought of sending again for Anthea, or for Fay; they might be able to help. He was looking through the papers taken from Lorne's pockets as the thought flashed through his mind, and putting aside some letter which might prove of interest. He did not lose himself in the task, for he had one ear open all the time. But the cries and her hysteria muffled the sound of the opening of the front door of the flat.

The first thing that attracted the Toff's attention was a sudden silence from Myra. He straightened up, looking towards the door. Then he heard a movement that sounded like a footstep. He moved towards the lounge, and was in time to see a man by the door, with his hand on the handle, and looking over his shoulder.

He was an undersized little man, with a burn-scar under his right eye – the man who had been with Lorne at the Queen's Hotel in Manchester.

In his right hand was a knife. He flung it.

The Toff saw it coming towards him, ducked, and fired from his pocket. The shot echoed loud and clear, while the bullet struck the man's thigh and brought him down. As he fell he began to cry, but the Toff was paying him no attention.

He was looking at Myra, who might have told him so much; but Myra was lying back in the chair, and with a vivid crescent of crimson about her neck.

Chapter Fifteen

The Man With The Scar

It had happened, and there was no purpose in accusing himself yet again of a sin of omission. Nor, as he stepped towards the woman and made sure that she was dead, did the Toff reproach himself. There was no way he could see in which he could have avoided this.

He let the limp hand go, and stepped to the door.

The man had stopped swearing. He did not look so much scared as vindictive, and when the Toff bent over him he kicked out with his uninjured leg. Rollison dodged the kick, yanked the man up, then carried him and let him fall on a settee. The blood was coming through the navy blue trousers. The Toff put a towel on the seat.

"Do you want first aid or don't you?"

"You can ruddy well do what yer ruddy well like!"

The Toff cut away a patch of trousers and swabbed the wound; the bullet had gone into the thigh, and probably touched the bone.

"You'll need a surgeon," said the Toff. "A police surgeon, too. What do they call you?"

"You won't git a word outa me!"

"Won't I, Benny?"

The man's surprise was ludicrous, and told the Toff that this was the Benny whom Lorne had mentioned; that was nearly conclusive evidence – judging from Lorne's conversation with Myra – that Benny had murdered the man at Grey Street. The knowledge was satisfying; the man's refusal to talk was not. There was no way in which the Toff could think of making him.

He telephoned Scotland Yard. McNab was not there, but an inspector promised to arrange for a police-surgeon and an ambulance to come at once.

Until their arrival Benny had maintained a sullen silence. On it he began to swear again, and nothing the inspector or the surgeon could do quietened him. The latter confirmed the need for an immediate operation for the removal of the bullet, and that the bone had been touched.

Benny continued to hurl blasphemies until he was carried out on a stretcher.

Detective-Inspector Wilson, young, spruce and eager, watched the middle-aged and uncommunicative surgeon examine Myra. He waited until the surgeon had pronounced his obvious verdict, asked questions about the bruises, and then had gone. By then the Toff had given Wilson the address at Dring Mansions; it would be better, now that Myra had been killed with such heartlessness, to bring Lorne in. He felt sick at the failure, but was not depressed for long, and the arrival of McNab cheered him.

McNab took the story on its face value, and seemed convinced that for once the Toff had told the whole truth. He did not even complain that the Toff should have told him of Lorne much earlier.

The Toff had not mentioned Harrison.

He hardly knew whether to be pleased or sorry when he was told that the police had found the flat empty, and that there had been all the signs of a hurried departure. He knew that a call would go out immediately for Lorne, while McNab had at least the satisfaction of getting the murderer of the woman.

But later that day, after the Toff had seen Anthea and Fay, but while nothing else had developed, McNab reported that Benny continued his refusal to talk. He denied everything despite the evidence against him, and he called the police and Rollison liars. He denied that he had ever been to Grey Street, and therein he made his second mistake.

He was identified by a ground-floor tenant at the flats of No. 14, and the time of his visit there coincided with the estimated hour of the first murder.

"And wi' that I'm satisfied we can fasten both crimes on him," said McNab, who called at the Toff's flat a little after seven o'clock, over a light meal, which the Toff arranged to be sent in from Fortnum's.

"So you're getting results," said Rollison slowly.

"And thanks t'ye, although we didn't know it," said McNab with some complacency. "But there's much we dinna know yet, Rolleeson. When we find Draycott—"

"What do you call the most important outstanding factors?"

McNab, in the middle of a grilled sole, considered.

"Well, shall we put Draycott's whereaboots first? And then the identity of the man killed at Grey Street. And finally the reason for the whole of it."

"You could do that," admitted the Toff.

He did not enlarge on his own opinions, chiefly because they were not yet properly formed. But when McNab had gone and he was alone he lay back in a chair and considered. He granted that McNab's three factors were important enough, but there were others which he added himself. They were:

1. Was the Mid-Provincial Building Society involved?
2. Were any of the Harveys involved?
3. What was Harrison's part in the affair?

When those questions and McNab's were answered there would be little to inquire about, but he also admitted that he was a long way from seeing the answers. He was cheered up a little when he learned, soon after McNab had gone back to the Yard to look at any reports which had come in, that the man Benny had been identified as Benjamin Kless, with an address in Shadwell.

Kless was not known to the police, but he might be to friends of Bert, and the Toff decided to visit the gymnasium. He had telephoned Fay that day, but had not seen her. Harrison had not put in an appearance; it was possible that he would keep out of the way, although the Toff hoped that he would think he had not been seen. Harrison might well prove the key to the whole affair. There were other problems, including the identity of Myra, but they were of lesser importance.

Jolly had not returned.

The Toff was hardly surprised at that, for Jolly would not come back until he was sure that he had discovered all that was worth learning about the cottage near the New Forest. He left a note in the kitchen, and just after ten o'clock left the flat and took a taxi to Mile Corner.

For the first time he saw that he was being followed.

He did not recognise the man, but a cab trailed him as far as Aldgate Pump, where his taxi was held up at the traffic lights, and from then onwards a small car had kept behind him. He suspected that it was being driven by a man who had in turn followed the second taxi. It was a youngish man, as far as he could see when the car passed beneath the lamps.

The Toff entered the Mile Corner just before closing-time.

Bert, a barrel-shaped man with a tremendous chest and width of shoulder, with an almost bald head and a slightly wheezy voice, was behind the bar. The arrival of the Toff, in lounge clothes that altered the expressions on the faces of some of the stevedores and labourers drinking there, made Bert's shining face shine even more in a smile of welcome. Within two minutes they were in a small parlour behind the bar, and Bert was pumping the Toff's hand.

"It's good t' see yer, Mr. Ar! I wasn't surprised, knowin' there was a bit o' su'thing up." Bert winked prodigiously. "My boys did yer a bit o' good, eh?"

So Bert had not had a confession from Manchester, and the Toff did not disillusion him. He thanked Bert gravely, and made inquiries about Kless. Bert had not heard of him, but he took Kless's address, and promised news by the following midday.

"Not a minnit later, s'welp me," said Bert earnestly. "Any-fink else I can do for you?"

"You can find me a change of clothes," said the Toff, and Bert widened his blue eyes.

"Goin' out an' about, are yer? Well, I can easy do that for yer, Mr. Ar."

It was not the first time that he had changed at Mile Corner. Bert had a small room at the top of the hotel where the Toff kept two or three suits of clothes that would have shocked his relatives. They were old and soiled and they made him look at one with the native inhabitants of the East End. Especially was he proud of a collection of brilliantly coloured caps, and he liked to take two or three with him when he went on his travels, so that he could change his cap, and thus improve the chance of being unobserved.

When he had changed, he used a box of grease-paints, which he also kept at the Corner, and a few deft lines at his eyes and mouth, with a little shading, altered the whole cast of his countenance. By day, and under a close scrutiny, it would not have passed muster. By night it made quite sure that no one would recognise him as the Toff.

Bert watched the transformation with growing amusement.

"Caw," he said, "yer a wonder—I'll say that, Mr. Ar! Bless me, I never saw anyone like it. A quarter of a bloomin' hour an' you ain't the same man. 'Ow yer do it I doan know. All set an' feelin' pritty?"

The Toff chuckled.

"All set, except that I want to borrow your car. I get worse, don't I?"

"Why, wot's easier'n that?" demanded Bert. "I'll go an' git it."

The Toff went down and sat at the wheel of a Model T Ford, a true antique. He could see the driver of the small Morris which had followed him from Aldgate under the light of a street lamp, and the man looked at his watch from time to time. It was nearly midnight before the Morris began to move, however, and the Toff slid his borrowed car after it.

Chapter Sixteen

Getting Warm

The Toff knew the chief cause of the trouble. He had not known when the case started, had been unable to get to the heart of it, and was compelled to keep following trails which might help him, yet might prove to be blind alleys.

As he drove behind the Morris, towards Aldgate, and presumably towards the centre of London, he reflected that during the past twenty-four hours Lorne had learned that Benny had not killed Draycott. At Manchester Lorne had believed that Draycott was dead, now he knew differently.

There were other things about Lorne worthy of attention.

At the moment of the returned visiting-card, the man had seemed to have qualities which could be admired but that was cancelled out by the murder of Myra. Whether she had played any vital part in the affair seemed unlikely.

Lorne had told her to 'go back where she belonged', of course, and had sneered that she would be well-off and out of danger. Well – many a woman had left a good home to consort with a rogue; and more often than not such *mésalliances* went wrong.

The Toff forgot Myra as he reached Piccadilly.

Theatre traffic had been thick enough to make reasonably sure that he was not seen following the other car, and he had had no difficulty doing the job mechanically. At Piccadilly, the other car beat him at the lights, and he was not sure which way it went. He took a chance, going round Piccadilly at a speed which policemen disliked; but the Toff saw his quarry speeding along Grosvenor Place. From there it reached Victoria, Ebury Bridge, Chelsea, and then Fulham.

It turned off New King's Road near Parson's Green.

There was little traffic, but two buses were between the Toff and the Morris, and that probably enabled the Toff to get through unseen. He turned down a side-turning, and saw the Morris parked outside a house which was one of a long series of terraces. The door opened and the driver was outlined against if for a moment, a sleek-looking youth, who was being admitted by a woman whose frizzy hair was also made into a silhouette by the hall light. The door closed then, and the Toff drove a few yards along, and left the car.

He walked back slowly to the house where his quarry had disappeared.

It was No. 18 Bruce Street. With that address firmly in his mind, he let the air out of two of the Morris's tyres, and opened the iron gate of the small front garden. Light was shining faintly at the front door, but he would not be able to force the lock without making a noise.

There was no light in the window on the right of the doorway, except that which was shining through from the hall, or another room. That was sufficient to show him the layout of the room, and that there was nothing near the window, which was tightly closed.

The catch was set, but the Toff was able to open it with a penknife. He slid the window up, wincing when it squeaked, but it was wide enough for him to get through at last. He stepped through, then stood for some seconds in the semi-darkness. He could hear voices from an upstairs room.

Then he heard a sharp cry from a woman or girl. There was a dull thud from the room above, and a woman's – or a girl's – voice came so clearly that it was impossible not to recognise it.

"I tell you he didn't!"

Fay Gretton was in this house.

* * *

It was the first real break that the Toff had received in this grim business, but it made up for many of the other disappointments. He learned of the capture of Fay only when he had found her.

He went into the hallway and walked softly up the stairs. He heard Lorne's voice.

"Don't keep lying to me. And if you shout I'll strangle you!"

Fay said nothing.

The Toff reached the landing and saw the door through which light was coming. It was strange that Lorne should risk trying to get information in a house where sound travelled so easily, and where every room had a window fairly close to the road or the houses in the adjoining street. He did not ponder long, but turned the handle of the door and opened it casually.

There was a shaded electric light, with Fay sitting on a chair – not bound or gagged, but sadly dishevelled and with the shoulder of her suit jacket torn. She was staring defiantly at Lorne and a smaller, swarthy man – the driver of the Morris – and if she was afraid she hid it well.

Lorne started to say: "I'll give you one more chance—" but before he could finish the Toff spoke in a rough voice that no one would have recognised as his: "Cut it out, you swine."

The big man swung round, and his companion turned, but neither moved further when they saw the gun in a hand that looked dirty even under the nails. With a peaked cap pulled over his eyes, and the rough clothes the Toff looked less like himself than a stevedore. His eyes were half hidden, and he spoke without opening his mouth much.

"Who the hell are you?" Lorne gasped.

"You'll learn," said the Toff. He saw the swarthy-faced man with Lorne, and now that he was at close quarters he fancied that he had seen him before, but he could not be sure where. "You git up," he said to Fay.

"It's one of those bloody prizefighters," the swarthy man said hoarsely.

"Keep yer mahth shut!" snapped the Toff, as Fay reached his side. He kept the gun on the others, but backed with Fay towards the door. He did not propose to take the slightest risk of injury to her.

He slipped out and closed the door.

He had taken the key out, and then he locked the door on them before hurrying down the stairs. By then Lorne had shouted in alarm or warning, and the door at the end of the ground-floor passage opened. From the front door the Toff saw a woman with frizzy grey hair. She called out in a high-pitched voice, but he did not catch the words. He opened the front door, and Fay went out swiftly, with him on her heels.

The door banged.

Then Rollison said in his normal voice: "Nice work, Fay! Now go and find a policeman or a call-box. Eighteen Bruce Street wants raiding in a hurry."

She gasped: *"Rolly!"*

"Get a move on!" urged the Toff, and blessed her when she turned and ran. He heard her high heels tapping the pavement, and moved back into shadows so that he could not be seen from the house opposite.

The door opened.

The woman came first, but Lorne pushed past her. The swarthy man slammed the door, which reverberated along the street. Lorne bundled into the Morris and pulled at the self-starter; the others climbed in at the back. As they did so the Toff walked towards the side of the car, which started abruptly, jolted, started again, and then stopped.

"A tyre's flat!" snarled Lorne. "Get out, all of you. There's a car further along. We'll take it."

"Oh no," said the Toff from the shadows. "That wouldn't do at all; it's mine."

Lorne said: "My God—Rollison!"

"Again," said the Toff. "I sent a friend, and there are others watching. Stay just where you are, all three of you."

Lorne gasped: "Now, listen, Rollison—"

"Later," said the Toff. "There are a lot of things I could do to hear from you, among them more of Myra and Benny. But for the moment stay where you are."

To them it must have been uncanny.

His voice came from the shadows, and they could not see him. Nor could they see others, but they imagined more were there. The Toff knew that they were trying to make up their minds to a sudden rush for safety, and yet were afraid that if they were outnumbered they would meet with disaster. He heard Lorne mutter under his breath, and the other man answer. The woman said clearly: "We can't do it."

"Shut your trap!" snarled Lorne.

And then things happened which the Toff had not expected.

It started when a car swung round the corner, with headlights full on, and bathing the whole street with light. In it the Toff was clearly visible, as was the fact that no one else was about. Lorne started to open the door. The Toff was prepared to shoot to stop him—

But a bullet came from the bigger car, close to his head!

He heard the thud as it hit the wall, and he ducked. He swung round, went through an open gateway and took cover in one of the shallow porchways of a house opposite No. 18. The shooting did not stop, but chipped pieces out of the bricks of the porch. The car slowed down, and he could hear but not see Lorne and the others scrambling into it.

Rollison fired for the tyres, but missed. Before he could shoot again the car gathered speed and swept towards the end of the road. As it passed Bert's car he saw a stab of flame and then another, and the tyres of the stationary car burst with loud reports that startled the residents of Bruce Street.

Windows were going up, and heads were thrust out. A man kept calling: "What's up there, what's up?"

Others added to the general din. Doors opened then, and two men came somewhat hesitantly into the street, but before they reached the Toff, or the Toff reached them, Fay and a policeman arrived from New King's Road. It was as well they had come late, for they might have been injured. But that was the only satisfaction

Rollison obtained, except the doubtful one of half an hour at Parson's Green Police Station with Fay, while his identity was established with the Yard. While he was waiting, 18 Bruce Street was entered by the police, but there were no papers of significance, and nothing to say where Lorne or the others might have gone.

The Toff did not ask questions as they were driven back to the West End. From his flat they telephoned Anthea, who proved to be frantic with anxiety, and who said she had been ringing the Toff at five-minute intervals. She promised to come round at once for Fay, who still looked dishevelled but showed little sign of her ordeal.

She had gone for a walk late that evening, and had been followed – she had thought by one of the boxers. But she had been hustled into a taxi, and a scarf had been used to gag her. She had lost consciousness, and come round in the house where the Toff had found her.

"It's so fantastic, Rolly. That blond brute wanted to know where Jimmy was. He thinks you know, and was sure you would have told me. Why *do* they want him?"

The Toff said, sombrely: "Because they don't like to think he's alive."

"But why on earth not?"

"I'm inclined to think that's the only question to matter. I—*blast* that 'phone!"

It was rare that he confounded the telephone, but it interrupted at a moment when he wanted to ask more questions of Anthea. He stepped to it, lifted it, and heard McNab's voice.

"Rolleeson, are ye there?"

"I think so," said the Toff.

"I want tae know what ye've been doing in Fulham, Rolleeson, but I've a wee bit of news ye'll want to hear yereself."

"I'm thirsting for it," said the Toff.

"Ye'll be surprised," said McNab, and paused, and then went on: "The woman Myra has been identified. She's Harvey's wife. Can you beat that?"

The Toff stared at Fay, who was on tenterhooks, and swallowed hard.

Myra was Phyllis Harvey's mother!

Chapter Seventeen

Burgle-Burgle

The Toff did not ask whether there was any possibility of mistake; he learned that both Phyllis Harvey, and Mortimer, her father, had seen and identified the body. Harvey had shown little or no emotion; the girl had swooned.

"Thanks for the call, Mac," the Toff said. "You'll find out what you can about the Bruce Street house."

"I will. It's a peety, Rolleeson, ye didna get the number of the big car which took Lorne away."

"I thought the same thing," the Toff said solemnly.

He returned to Fay, and told her, simply, and although she was surprised she was not appalled. She had known that Harvey and his wife did not get on well, and in fact had told the Toff.

"Now it's beginning to look as if Lorne enticed Myra from her husband because he needed her help. But no woman would leave her husband without a good reason."

Fay said quietly: "Harvey is a sarcastic beast."

"Sarcasm on its own is hardly enough for separation," said the Toff. "Slowly and surely we move towards the heart of this affair—the Mid-Provincial Building Society, or something connected with it."

"Can you be sure?"

"I can think I'm sure," said the Toff. "In the first place, Draycott, who has just lost an agency for it, disappears, and is in danger of murder. In the second, Lorne has an affair with Harvey's wife, clearly to obtain information. Lorne is the man who thought he had arranged for Draycott's murder, and that connects the two factors. Harvey, as the retired director, is a common denominator. The shares I found in Lorne's safe may or may not implicate Murray and Firth, the firm which won the agency from Draycott, but it will be as well if they answer some questions."

"Will the police ask them?"

The Toff regarded her with one eyebrow raised a little above the other.

"The police may or may not believe that Mid-Provincial are playing a large if indirect part, and probably know nothing of Draycott's loss of the agency. By the way, you were at the office today?"

"Of course. Things were much the same."

"What do the other staff think?"

"That Jimmy's away on business. The police were there last night, apparently, but the rest of the staff don't know why."

"Which is McNab being cunning," ruminated the Toff. "Will you think it breaking faith if you let me see the correspondence of the Murray-Firth-Mid-Provincial argument?"

"No, but I don't think it will do much good. I know the file well. It's quite ordinary. When do you want to see it?"

"Now," said the Toff.

"Tonight I—oh, well," said Fay, and she smiled. "I'll have to tidy myself up a bit."

She was doing her hair when Anthea arrived with Jamie. Jamie was clearly determined to act the knight errant until the danger was over. The Toff was puzzled by the failure of Bert's men to keep Fay watched, and he hoped that nothing had happened to them.

As if to answer his unspoken queries, Bert telephoned. He was in a most apologetic mood, for he had heard from Manchester. He was a little reproachful, for he considered that Mr. Ar should have told him the truth, and he said earnestly that he would not have had it happen for the world. And then there was something just as bad. Tibby Mendoz – Mr. Ar would remember Tibby; he was the promising little lightweight who had been at the Ring several times – had been watching 1023 Bayswater Road. He had been persuaded to leave his post for five minutes, been hit over the head, and delivered to his home address some hours later. For a while he had been nervous of advising Bert, but at last had plucked up courage to do so.

"I wouldn't have 'ad it happen," said Bert with a fine mixture of aspirates, "fer the world, Mr. Ar. Did I give Tibby a dressin'down!"

"Go easy with him," pleaded the Toff. "It might have been a lot worse, Bert. I'll get you to send him and another man back to the house. In a couple of hours from now will do. All right?"

"You betcher life."

"Good man," said the Toff. "And I'm more than ever anxious to hear what you can find about Kless."

"Okay," said Bert.

"And then there's a man in this who might be an Italian. Short, slim, marcelled hair—you know the type. Keep your eyes open for him, Bert, and tell the watchers at Bayswater Road to be wary of him."

"Right y'are," said Bert.

The Toff thanked him and rang off. He did not explain in any detail to Jamie, but Anthea and Jamie insisted on joining the expedition.

"It's all right with me," said the Toff, "but the police might not agree, and they'll almost certainly be watching."

But it appeared that they were not.

Fay had the keys of the office, and was able to get in without any question from waiting policemen. The Toff watched the outside of the tall office building where Draycott ran his business, but saw no one who might be a policeman. He looked about the small outer office. There were four rooms, three very small and the other much larger, where Draycott and Fay worked. The furniture was not new, but neither was it old. The filing system was on modern lines, and in steel cabinets. About the office there was a suggestion that Draycott's business was flourishing.

A small vase of roses was on Fay's desk.

She obtained the Mid-Provincial file for the Toff, and he sat at Draycott's desk and looked through the more recent correspondence. He hoped to find something which might suggest why Draycott was frightened. After twenty minutes Anthea grew restless.

"Do we have to stay here all night, Rolly?"

The Toff smiled.

"You invited yourself, my sweet, but far be it from me to detain you. Fay, did Draycott keep a personal file here?"

"Yes, in his desk."

"Have you a key?"

"No," said Fay, but she indicated the drawer where the Toff would find it. Then for the first time Jamie and Anthea felt that there was interest in the evening, and they watched him insert a thin blade of his knife, and do strange things to the lock of the drawer. It clicked back after several minutes of manipulation, and Anthea said: "What a good thing you're not a thief, Rolly!"

"How do you know I'm not?" demanded the Toff.

He ran through the files in the drawer. He knew that Fay was also watching, and he was not surprised when he said after a few seconds: "It's not there now."

"I was afraid not," said the Toff. "The inference is that he took it with him, although of course it might have been stolen. Oh, well. We'd better call it a day, although it might be an idea if I looked through these papers. I—oh, damn I" broke off the Toff. "I'm suffering from colour-blindness. The police have searched this thoroughly, of course."

"Meaning they might have taken the file?"

"It could be." Rollison shrugged and stood up. He looked weary, and more than a little disgruntled. "I think—"

Then he stopped.

The other wondered why he was looking towards the outer door, but they did not wonder for long, for they too heard the noise at the lock, a scratching sound suggesting that someone was trying to emulate the Toff and get in where he should not without a key. The Toff said sharply: "Keep quiet, all of you. I'm going to put out the light."

The door leading to the outer office was closed, and it was not likely that any light showed into the passage. The switch went up, and they waited with bated breath in the darkness. *Sotto voce* the Toff instructed them to stay exactly where they were, and told them that he was going to the outer office. They did not hear him move, but they could still hear the noise at the door.

Then came a sharp click!

They were on tenterhooks, while the Toff – just behind the door, and where he would not be seen when it was opened – waited eagerly.

The door creaked as it opened.

There was a moment of silence before a light was switched on. It made the Toff blink, but although it shone through into the other office it did not show the three waiting there.

A man stood there, a man who started to close the door. The Toff saw his hand, and kept his own hand in his pocket with the fingers about the gun. The door closed softly, and the Toff saw the intruder.

Jolly had returned from his quest in Hampshire; and had burglariously entered the office of James Draycott!

Chapter Eighteen

News From Hampshire

For a fraction of a second Jolly looked astounded. His lined face had an expression of acute wariness, and his left hand was close to his hip pocket. Then he saw and heard the Toff, and the wariness disappeared; his face became set.

"Good evening, sir," said Jolly politely.

"Jolly! What the devil are you doing here?"

Jolly lifted one hand as if in self-defence.

"I am sorry to have unwittingly raised your hopes, sir, but I assure you that I had no idea that I would find you in the office. I have been to the flat, to find neither you nor a message. I thereupon did what I considered to be the safer course."

"Less verbiage," ordered the Toff.

"Very good sir. I have returned from Hampshire within the past hour, with information that might be of interest."

From the other room Fay said: "Thank heavens for that!"

Jolly turned abruptly, and the Toff led him into the other office, and Jolly recovered, bowed, apologised for any fright which he may have caused the trio, and then went on to tell his story in a precise if somewhat pedantic fashion.

He had reached Allen Cottage, to find that the place was empty, and a 'To Let, Furnished' notice attached to the front gate. Consequently he had obtained keys from the nearest house agent in Romsey. The cottage, a small one of five rooms, had been to let for some time; but Jolly had found conclusive evidence that it had recently been occupied.

There had been a smell of comparatively fresh tobacco-smoke in one room. In the kitchen it was possible to smell fat which had clearly been used for frying within the past twelve hours. A bed had been slept in, and there had been a number of cigarette-ends about, all of which had been somewhat carelessly disposed—some in the fireplace but many on the floor.

"We'll pass the carelessness of the illegal tenant," said the Toff. "Have you any of the ends?"

"Of course, sir." Jolly took a small envelope from his pocket and handed it to the Toff, who took out cigarette-ends contained in it while Jolly went on with his story.

In the hope that the unlawful tenant would return, he had stayed in or near the cottage for the rest of the day. He had seen no one, but towards dusk he had decided that he should with advantage search the place more thoroughly. And behind the bed which had been slept in, and was also still dishevelled, he had found an envelope screwed up and thrown carelessly away, with a note inside it which Jolly handed to the Toff.

Fay, Anthea and Jamie crowded him to read it.

Fay exclaimed sharply: "It's Draycott's writing!"

"That's reasonable evidence that he's been to Allen Cottage," said the Toff thoughtfully, "and that he's a long way from dead. It's addressed to you!" He stopped, and then read:

"*Dear Fay,*
"*You will find the key of my desk in an envelope in the front of the 'For Sale' filing cabinet. Please open the desk, take out my 'Private' file and send it to—*"

There the letter stopped.

It was not dated, and it was not completed. It was screwed up as if Draycott had decided half-way through that it was useless to write it; and because of it Jolly had decided to lose no time at all in trying to get the file.

"And you were quite right," said the Toff. "It's a pity the file is missing."

Jolly stared.

"Indeed it is, sir. I had no idea—"

"You saw none of McNab's men outside, did you?"

"I was surprised by their absence, sir. I was, in fact, quite prepared for the need for a little evasion."

"It isn't like McNab to miss the obvious or to do anything careless. And obviously Draycott might try to come back here."

"Why, if he's safe in his Hampshire place?" asked Jamie.

"For the file," said the Toff. "He wanted it, or he would not have started to write to Fay. It's clear that he decided a letter was neither wise nor safe, and decided to try to get the file himself. The fact that it's missing makes it possible he succeeded."

"I wonder if he has," exclaimed Fay. "And I wonder if he could have 'phoned when I was away from the office?"

"The staff would have told you," said the Toff. When they reached Jamie's house the Toff saw Mr. Tibby Mendoz, small and wellknit, and very apologetic about his bang over the head. He assured the Toff – and – Fay – that it would not happen again, and said also that Bert had sent his, Tibby's, brother with him. Two others would relieve them at dawn.

"Rolly, you really think I need watching like this?" Fay asked.

"After tonight, don't you?"

"I—I suppose so. But why?"

"Lorne thinks you know where Jimmy is," said Anthea.

"But can that be the only thing?"

"If you can think up another motive," said the Toff, "let me know. Now I'm going. I've a feeling that we won't want to be tired in the morning."

It was half past two when he reached Gresham Terrace. On the way, and for ten minutes while they were preparing for bed, Jolly went into further details about his trip, but he could offer no further information. He was a little uncertain as to his wisdom in returning, but he had telephoned twice and found the Toff away: he had considered that it was essential for him to try to get the private file, and had been guided by that. The Toff arranged for Jolly to make a third trip to Hampshire on the following morning.

"What kind of place is it, Jolly?"

"Most charming, sir."

"And the furniture?"

"It could not be called ideal, but there is nothing which you would find disturbing, sir."

"Is it any better than the cottages you inspected the day before?"

"It is superior to any, sir. In fact had I seen it the day before I would have obtained an option then. Instead I obtained one today, paying twenty-five pounds to represent the first month's rent and all agreement charges and other incidentals. The rent is twelve guineas a week, sir: it is moderate for the place. I trust," called Jolly into a silence that was broken by the Toff getting into bed, "my action meets with your approval, sir?"

The Toff called back: "I am beginning to think the saying that no man is indispensable is all wrong. It meets with my full approval. And as far as we can tell, Draycott is using a cottage as a hiding-place which I have undertaken to rent through you."

"You have the option, yes."

"I see," said the Toff. A minute afterwards he added sleepily: "I wonder what McNab will think when he finds out? And I wonder— oh, damn! I meant to ring the Yard about the absence of surveillance on Draycott's office." The bed creaked again, and then Jolly heard the 'ting' of the telephone. When a night-operator spoke from the Yard, McNab was not there, and Wilson was also off duty, but a Sergeant Kain was acting for them.

Kain, a large man and one of the old school, sceptical of Hendon College and its professed advantages, heard the Toff out and then said stolidly: "You're wrong sir. There are two men watching the offices. I stationed them there myself."

"They didn't stop me going in," said the Toff.

"Why should they, sir? They were watching for Draycott."

The Toff agreed that was reasonable. He had done what he felt necessary, replaced the receiver and went to sleep.

He dreamed of Fay and Draycott, and Draycott was a peculiar mixture, in that fantasy, of Harvey's secretary, Ted Harrison, Jamie Fraser, and Chief Inspector McNab.

Next morning, he decided to see Phyllis Harvey first, and presented himself at the St. John's Wood house just after eleven o'clock.

A small car stood outside, but beyond giving it a cursory glance the Toff thought nothing of it. He pulled his Frazer-Nash behind it, rang the front-door bell, and was admitted by a middle-aged woman in maid's dress. She looked pale and harassed, and her eyes were lack-lustre and red-rimmed.

"Good morning," said the Toff. "May I see Miss Harvey, please?"

The woman burst into tears.

It was so completely unexpected that the Toff could only stand and stare. But then he spoke sharply, and she dabbed an already damp handkerchief at her eyes, apologised, and said in a voice that was very unsteady: "She's—she's been taken away by the police, sir."

"She's been *arrested?*"

"Yes, yes, sir, that's it; a sweeter, lovelier lady there never was, and now she's been taken away!" More tears threatened, while the Toff stood at a loss. He decided to try to see Harvey, but his thoughts of Harvey faded when a door opened at the head of the stairs, and he heard a surly voice say: "It's a lot of nonsense, but it can't be helped. I'll call again, sir."

The door closed, and Edward Harrison came hurrying down the stairs.

Chapter Nineteen

McNab In High Fettle

The Toff stood by the side of the maid, who was sniffing, while Harrison came hurrying down the stairs in a self-important manner which the Toff had once been able to tolerate, but which now irritated him. The cricketer was frowning, looking as if he carried all the troubles of the world on his shoulders, and his lanky frame was for once clad in a respectable-looking grey suit. His glasses were perched too far down the bridge of his nose, which may have accounted for the fact that he was within two yards of the Toff before he recognised him.

Harrison pulled up sharply.

For a moment, and only for a moment, he was off his balance. His mouth opened, and then shut tightly. Then he spoke sharply, and in a rather querulous, dissatisfied manner, that of a man for whom things were not running smoothly.

"Oh, it's you, is it?" he said. "What the deuce are you doing here? Aren't you satisfied with the havoc you've caused?"

"Did anyone ever tan your hide when you were young?" asked Rollison tartly.

Harrison glowered.

"I haven't any time for being smart with you."

"I have grave doubts whether you will ever be smart with anyone," said the Toff.

It looked as if Harrison would start a row.

It seemed to the Toff that he was very short on sleep, and that his nerves were not in good order.

Harrison changed his mind.

"All right," he growled. "There's no need to get on your high horse. If you'd had the tousing I have in the last day or two you wouldn't be so sweet-tempered. What *are* you doing here, anyway?"

"I'd come for a talk with Miss Harvey."

"You'd *what!*" Harrison barked. "Well, well. The great Rollison is outwitted by the police, is he? They arrested her without asking your permission. I thought you had them eating out of your hand."

"You mix too much fancy with fact," the Toff said. "Is Harvey in?"

"Yes, but he isn't likely to see you."

"Well," said the Toff, "I can at least try."

He turned away from Harrison and went up the stairs, reached the landing and then the door from which Harrison had come. He tapped, perfunctorily, and opened it.

He saw Mortimer Harvey for the second time, and was affected most by the man's arrogant expression. Harvey was tall and well-built, and probably nearly sixty, although he looked younger. His hair was no more than iron grey, and his grey eyes were cold but not unattractive. His fresh-coloured skin had a suggestion of the open air, and his large but regular features – the mouth particularly large and yet well-shaped – combined to give the impression that he had neither time nor patience for lesser men.

He was sitting at a large wooden desk in a study lined with books. The carpet was thick, the oak panelling modern and expensive, and the general furnishings of the room were luxurious. There was a cigar in Harvey's right hand, and in his left a sheaf of papers. He was saying "Who's that?" as the Toff went in, and he frowned when the door opened.

"Who are you?"

"My name," said the Toff, "is Rollison."

He took a card from his pocket and laid it face upwards in front of Harvey. He stood quite still by the desk, and Harvey did not trouble to look at the card. His face lost a little of its high colour.

"Oh," he said, and although his voice was mellow it had then a harsh, almost a threatening, note. "So you're Rollison. And you have the infernal impertinence to come here? Don't stay, *Mr.* Rollison. I am quite prepared to have you thrown out."

The door opened again, and the Toff knew that it was Harrison, but he did not turn round.

"Wouldn't it be wise to think again?"

"No," said Harvey harshly. "I've nothing to say to you that would make pleasant hearing. My God!" he added, and pushed his chair back and lifted a hand as if prepared to strike the Toff then. "I've half a mind to thrash you myself!"

"All of which is nonsense, and I think you know it. Come right in, Harrison, don't stand by the door. Now—" The Toff regarded Harvey coldly, as he sat on the edge of the desk. He appeared to take it for granted that he had every right to be there. "Are you suggesting that Miss Harvey's detention is due to me?"

"I know it is!"

"You've either been misled or you're lying," said the Toff, and there was every intention in his mind to anger the other man. "Of the two, I'm inclined to think that the latter is the right solution."

"Of all the infernal nerve!" exclaimed Harrison, who had lined himself alongside Harvey.

"Oh yes," said the Toff, "I've a nerve all right. Sometimes when it's as well. I'm matched and nearly outmatched for nerve. I have seen your daughter twice, only once to speak to. I have not discussed my meeting with her with the police."

"That's a lie!" snapped Harrison. "I know that you told them she could find Draycott if she wanted to."

"Oh?" said the Toff, and he turned the word into a wealth of disbelief. "So you've been convincing Harvey that I'm the bad man of the piece, have you?"

"You know very well that's true."

"There's neither time nor need for a lot of argument," the Toff said. "Harvey, your wife was killed in my flat, when I was about to talk to her. I had hoped that I was in time to save her from further unpleasant experiences, and I am quite sure that I saved her life on one occasion. Does that interest you?"

Harvey said in a strained voice: "Nothing about my wife interests me. I had not seen her for some weeks."

"Weeks?" asked the Toff, and sounded surprised. "That isn't long for—but that's hardly what I'm here for. Did you know Lorne?"

Harvey said: "I knew him as a *roué* and a rogue. I warned Myra" – he paused after using his wife's name, and went on in a harsher voice – "and I told her the inevitable consequences of consorting with him. She refused to take my advice."

"When did you first meet Lorne?" asked the Toff.

"Some years ago."

"As a business associate?"

"What is this? An inquisition?" demanded Harrison, and he was breathing heavily.

"You be quiet," said the Toff, with a sharp authority. "Mr. Harvey, I would appreciate an answer. Whatever is happening, whatever personal anxieties the present affair may have caused you, they are incidental to a larger issue in which Lorne figures prominently. It is essential to know all about the man, particularly if your daughter is to be saved from even more distressing experiences than she has already suffered." Harrison muttered, hardly above a whisper: "It's a lot of nonsense."

Harvey said slowly, and with his eyes on the Toff: "I met Lorne some four years ago, in connection with a business transaction. Harrison introduced us."

"Oh," said the Toff very gently, and again: "Oh. You introduced Lorne, did you?" He glanced at Harrison, whose face was very pale. "I'd no idea that you had met before. You omitted to mention that at Manchester, didn't you? And afterwards?"

"There wasn't any need to. I'd discovered what a rogue he was, and I've had nothing to do with him for a year or more."

It was possible that this was his best opportunity of telling Harrison about seeing him at Lorne's flat; but he let it pass.

"There are things the police would like to know from you, I think. We'll go to the Yard, Harrison."

"I'm damned if I will!"

"You needn't be damned yet," said the Toff. "Excuse us, Mr. Harvey."

There followed one of those remarkable things of which the Toff was capable. He stepped to Harrison's side and gripped his forearm, and Harrison found that he had to move to escape the sharp pain that ran up his arm. Harvey was about to protest when the Toff reached the door, opened it, propelled Harrison quickly along the passage. Harrison was forced along at such a rate that he could not stop, while in the study Harvey was staring at the door.

The Toff took Harrison out of the front door and sat him with force into the Frazer-Nash. Harrison was rubbing at his arm and swearing under his breath, but made no attempt to get away. The Toff was pleased with that as he made for Westminster. In the St. John's Wood house Harvey kept staring at the desk. At last he picked up the Toff's card, and it was almost by accident that he turned it over. He saw the pencilled drawings of the top hat, the monocle and the swagger-cane, and he started; and then he stared at it fixedly, with the colour draining from his face.

The Toff pulled the Frazer-Nash up outside the Embankment gates of Scotland Yard and looked unpleasantly at Harrison.

"Well, are you going to tell your story?"

"I—I don't give a damn what I tell I" snapped Harrison. "I didn't have to tell you that I'd done business with Lorne, did I? You're taking a lot too much on yourself, Rollison. I—"

And then he struck at the Toff.

The blow that slid off the Toff's chin, for he was expecting it and he moved his head. But he pretended to be off his balance for a moment, and Harrison took his long legs over the side of the small car and ran for a taxi that was cruising past. He jumped in while it was moving, to the astonishment of several policemen and passers-by. And as the cab gathered speed the Toff smiled obscurely before turning into the Yard.

McNab was alone in the large office, and at the Toff's appearance he smiled widely. He also spoke with warmth, and stood up to pull a chair forward for the Toff.

"Well, well, Rolleeson! I'm glad ye've come—I was on the 'phone to ye only half an hour ago."

"Nice of you," said the Toff. "The idea, of course, was to tell me about Miss Harvey's arrest."

"Well, to mention it," said McNab, and beamed. "Ye've been slower than ye often are on this business, Rolleeson. Ye've been trying to put more than there was into it. Och, I'm not blaming ye—dinna think that for a moment. But from the first it was clear to me that Draycott had killed yon body at the flat and was in hiding. That's what happened, ye ken."

"So? You've got Draycott?"

"I will have when his lassie talks."

"And you're going to charge her as an accessory?"

"I think so," said McNab. "Now, Rolleeson, dinna ye start getting fidgety, mon. I can see that ye're going to ask me where the murder of Myra Harvey comes in, but I've all that worked out. I can tell ye the whole story, if ye'll listen."

"I'm listening," said the Toff.

"Good! Well, now, it's like this. Harvey was being blackmailed because of the association of his wife with the man Lorne, ye ken. Draycott knew of it, and brought the blackmailer to his flat and killed him there. That made Draycott run, but he told the lassie where he would be. That's one part. The other is that Lorne was behind the blackmailing, Rolleeson. The blackmailer worked for him, and Harvey's wife learned of it. When ye took her away Lorne was afraid she would talk, and he sent the prisoner to make sure she didna. The prisoner made a mistake in trying where he did; we owe his capture to ye, Rolleeson, and I'm grateful. But when we've got Lorne and Draycott we'll have them all. It was complicated," added McNab complacently, "but it works out. Can ye see anything the matter with the reasoning?"

"And you're really going to build your case on that?" The Toff asked incredulously.

"Of course I am." McNab spoke sharply.

"There are times when you positively frighten me," said the Toff. "And the worst trouble is," he added, in his eyes an almost haunted look, "I don't see that I can prove you wrong just yet."

Chapter Twenty

And Out Of Temper

As the Toff had spoken the smile had disappeared from the Chief Inspector's face, and by the time the Toff had finished McNab was glowering.

"You're talking nonsense."

"You think so?" said the Toff, and stood up. "Mac, it's a beautiful picture, a lovely story that holds together in parts, and might conceivably please your Assistant Commissioner. But if you act on it, if you get Draycott and Lorne and work on the basis of your theory, you're going to make one of the mistakes of your life."

"I think that I can be the judge of that," said McNab coldly.

"You think you can," agreed the Toff. "The trouble is you can be the judge, and there's no one to stop you working on it your way. But you mustn't do it, Mac."

"To suit some fool idea that ye've got?" said McNab. "I won't do it. I've the warrant for Draycott's arrest these past three days, and the call for Lorne went out last night. When I've got them both I've got everything."

"I'll go, Mac. I'll go a long way away, and if it weren't for the fact that you're proposing to try to hang two innocent people I'd go for good. But whatever you do, remember I've warned you. You might give the right men the time they need to get away with their job."

"I've nothing more to say," said McNab.

The Toff, who was rarely so out of temper, left the office knowing that he could have smoothed McNab down.

He went at once to the offices of Draycott and Company. Fay was given his name, and she was standing up, eager-faced, when he entered her office.

"Any luck, Rolly?"

"I'm sorry, Fay," he said. "I have just come from the police, and we are mutually unpopular. They've arrested Phyllis Harvey."

"My goodness!" said Fay, and sat down abruptly.

As she sat she knocked against the vase of roses on her desk. The water spread over the carpet, and the roses spilled in all directions. The Toff went down on his knees to pick up the flowers, while Fay took a duster from her desk and mopped up the water. It took several minutes, and the Toff regained much of his equanimity. He was smiling when the flowers were back on the desk.

In bending down Fay's hair had become untidy, and as she brushed it back from her forehead, dark waves that were smooth and glossy in a shaft of sunlight coming through the window, the Toff acknowledged that there was a breathless loveliness about Fay which was not beauty, but something even greater.

"You've heard nothing more, I suppose?"

"I was hoping there would be a call or a letter from Jimmy, but there's nothing at all."

"I see," said the Toff. "There are things we may be able to do. Can you get me a list of the partners of Murray and Firth, and another of the directors of the Mid-Provincial Building Society?"

"Yes, but it will take some time."

"This evening will do," said the Toff. "If you do get word from Draycott, tell him to stay in hiding, but not to return to Allen Cottage."

Fay nodded.

"One way and the other," said the Toff, "I almost wish there was no Jimmy."

Her cheeks lost colour, and he had further evidence of what she felt for Jimmy Draycott. But she cheered up considerably before he left the office, and promised to get the information quickly.

Rollison telephoned the agents in Romsey who had given Jolly the option on Allen Cottage. There was no telephone installed, although the wiring had been done and it would only be a day or two before the instrument could be fitted. The Toff arranged for them to take a message to Jolly, and was at some pains to concoct one that gave nothing away. He was satisfied that Jolly would get the message before the police reached the cottage. That Phyllis Harvey would, under slight pressure, divulge the address which Draycott had given her was as nearly certain as the fact that the sun shone in the heavens.

Next, the Toff made his way to Mile Corner.

He had seen Bat Mendoz, Tibby's brother, outside the office of Draycott and Company, and he felt sure that Fay was being carefully watched. He was thoughtful as he drove through the thick East End traffic towards Aldgate, and then along the Mile End Road. The public house was open, as was the gymnasium at the back. When the Toff went to the latter he saw Bert, in shirt-sleeves and smoking a shining new pipe, leaning on one post of a ring, while two lightweights danced and frolicked about on the canvas. Bert was deep in his self-appointed task.

"Keep that *left* movin', can't yer—don't dance like a chorus gel, Skiff, this ain't a ballroom, it's a boxing-ring. Now hit him —hit him! That's—*Why, Mr. Ar!*'

The pounding of feet on the sawdust-covered canvas and the occasional slap of a large glove on a face or a glistening chest punctuated the conversation for the next five minutes. Bert had no positive information about the man named Kless, but was expecting word within the next half-hour. If Mr. Ar would wait, maybe it would arrive. Rollison said that he would.

"That's ri'," said Bert. "No use givin' *you* arf a story, I always think that. No more trouble, I 'ope?"

"Lashings of trouble," said the Toff.

"Oh, dear," said Bert surprisingly. "You look a bit orf, if you ask me. Things goin' wrong, are they?" Bert made a clicking noise of sympathy. "They're always doin' that, Mr. Ar. Take these boys o' mine. You get them up to a point where you reckon they'll take anything that comes, an' the first time you put 'em in a prize-ring—bah!" exclaimed Bert. "They loses their nerve, an' they flops."

"'Flops' is expressive," said the Toff.

For once he obtained no pleasure from watching the youngsters in the ring, nor from Bert's colourful conversation. As it happened, there was not long to wait, for there was a sudden flurry at the entrance to the gymnasium, and a short man with powerful shoulders, one and a half cauliflower ears, a broken nose, square lips that had been sadly battered at frequent intervals, and a pair of the merriest blue eyes that ever shone from an Irishman, approached Bert and the Toff. "Back, then, Pat?" said Bert.

"Why, shure Oi'm back," said Patrick Mullen, one-time lightweight champion of Great Britain, "and it's glad Oi am to see Mr. Ar, as iver was." He shook hands warmly, and told what he had learned graphically.

What with the police watching 91 Gay Street, Bethnal Green, and an old shrew of a woman he had learned to be Kless's mother, it had not been easy. But that had not deterred Patrick Mullen, who had slipped over the back-garden wall – garden meant a small concrete-covered yard – under the very eyes of the police, and put the fear of death into Old Mother Kless. She had, it seemed, two sons; they kept her in gin and other things, but they had been missing for a day or more. One was Grab, who, the police said, had thrown himself out of a railway train, which she did not believe; and the other was Benny. "Benny!" exclaimed the Toff. Pat Mullen beamed.

"Och, Benny she said, an' she wouldn't lie to me, Mr. Ar, Oi'll assure ye of that. And then there were her lodgers." The Toff said sharply: "Go on."

"A big man, fair as a Scotsman," said Mullen, "and another nasty little wop, the one ye told Tibby to watch for, Oi would not mind swearing if I swore at all, which I niver did an' niver will, the saints forgive me. They've been living there at odd times for a year, Mr. Ar, sometimes only staying for a night or two and sometimes a week, but always paying her. Which they havin't done for a month, she says, and she gets no pleasure from it."

"Have the police been at her?" asked the Toff. "At her! Oi'll say she's raving good and mighty at thim, but she'll niver say a word," said Patrick. "She's loyal in her way, and she hates the police, and Oi for one don't blame her. It cost me a pound as ever was and all the oaths I know that I wouldn't let on, Mr. Ar."

"That's fine." The Toff repaid the pound but not a penny more, for that would have given offence. "Bert, I want Ma Kless and her house watched closely. Will you make sure of that?"

"Why, sure," said Bert.

"And I'll try to have a look at her tonight," went on the Toff. "I want the big blond man or the little wop put away somewhere so that I can talk to them if they show up, but they won't while the police are watching."

"You only 'ave to say the word, Mr. Ar. The dicks won't know we're watching, neither."

"Keep at it, Bert," Rollison said. "You're the best."

He went off a few minutes afterwards, while Bert arranged for Ma Kless to be kept under close surveillance. Bert, and others like him in the East End, explained the power and the legend which had spread about the Toff, and the reason why he could so often do more than the police. There was little chance of the police getting information, for the ranks of the East End closed against them, and only a copper's nark stood any chance of giving them news; but the life of a nark was no sinecure, and his story was often only half true and usually late.

The Toff could and did get vital information, and frequently acted on it.

Back at Gresham Street he was thinking with satisfaction of the fact that Lorne and the little man he had followed to Fulham were lodgers at the house of Grab and Benny Kless. Grab was the man who had killed himself, and Benny the murderer of Myra Harvey: so much was certain.

And it was likely that they would return once the police lost interest in the house.

For the first time he felt that he was moving in the right direction but it did not cheer him much, for he was still worried by the possibility of the police finding Draycott formulating a charge which might ruin Draycott. He was still thinking that when he entered the flat, to hear the telephone ringing. He picked it up, and he heard Jolly's voice.

"I am glad you have returned, sir," said Jolly. "I have been trying to get you for some time. Mr. Draycott is here. I thought you would like to know."

Chapter Twenty-One

Draycott In The Flesh

Even from a master of understatement that made the Toff gulp; but he was not affected for long, and he said sharply: "At the cottage, Jolly?"

"Yes, sir."

"Is he all right?"

"He is somewhat out of temper but otherwise I do not think that he can complain."

"All right. I'll come down at once, but you're to leave the cottage immediately. You've had my message?"

"Yes, sir. And I have made arrangements. There is another small place, a bungalow, sir" – Jolly appeared to sniff – "some half a mile from here. It is empty, but I have persuaded Mr. Draycott for the time being that it will be wise to stay there. Is that in order?"

"Give me the address and directions for reaching the bungalow," said the Toff, "and do nothing that might make either of you conspicuous. I expect McNab down there at any time."

"I shall have the situation well in hand, sir."

"Right," said the Toff, and he rang off.

He did not lose much time in going from the flat and taking the Frazer-Nash from the garage. He watched the road behind him, but did not think he was followed. That did not prevent him from being watchful, but it was not until he was on the other side of Winchester that he had any reward.

A small car pulled out of a side-road and turned after him. The Toff could see the face of the driver in his mirror; and he knew that it was the little man who had led him to Fulham, and afterwards escaped with Lorne and the grey-haired woman. He was cheered by the discovery, and yet puzzled. The man had certainly not followed him from London, but must have been stationed in the by-road after receiving a report that he was on the way.

Suddenly the Toff said aloud: "My only aunt, *am* I sane? They've been watching Jolly. Of course they've been watching Jolly!"

He did not try to shake his man off, but went to Allen Cottage. The place was shut up, and the 'To Let, Furnished' notice was still fastened to the gate. He looked under a door-mat in the porch, and found the key; Jolly had left it in case he called there.

He went inside, and lost no time going upstairs. From the front bedroom window he saw his follower. The man had drawn his car up a hundred yards along a narrow lane, where the cottage and a bungalow were situated – some half a mile apart. The turning was off the main Romsey-Southampton Road.

The driver walked slowly and silently up the narrow garden path.

The Toff went as silently downstairs with a hand at his pocket, and stepped towards the front door, which he had left ajar. He could hear the rustle of the other's movement, and as he went behind the door it was pushed open an inch; another, then wide enough for the man to step through.

"Come right in," invited the Toff.

The man whirled about, but the gun in the Toff's hand stopped him from going for his own. Rollison left nothing to chance. He hit his man on the point, finding the nerve-centre that brought unconsciousness in a wink. He stopped him from falling, lowered him to the ground, and then ran through his pockets.

He did not stop to look at what he had found, but lifted the man, who was no more than five-feet-three or four, and light with it, to a small kitchen. Then he opened the back door and carried his burden out.

The cottage was not overlooked, for the bungalow was the nearest building. But not far away were trees, and a field in which cows were grazing. There was a deep ditch alongside the hedge, and the Toff worked fast. With cord he had brought with him he bound the man's ankles and wrists, and with a handkerchief he gagged him. Then he tumbled him into the ditch – which was on the side of the hedge away from the cottage – and pulled a branch of a beech tree that had fallen near by so that it covered his prisoner completely.

Then he moved to the car, a Morris.

He first drove this as far as the bungalow, then returned for the Frazer-Nash, driving that into the garden of the bungalow, out of sight of the road. It would not have to stay there indefinitely, but for the time being was sufficiently under cover.

He had finished when he saw a car draw up outside the cottage. He was behind the hedge of the bungalow garden when it arrived, and he could not be seen. He saw McNab and Sergeant Wilson step out, and he watched them walk towards the front door.

He smiled obscurely as he turned to the bungalow, and was about to tap on the bungalow door when it opened and he saw Jolly. Then he saw Jimmy Draycott for the first time.

* * *

For the Toff it was a strange moment. His only picture of Draycott had been through Fay, and that had been biased. There was no preconceived notion in the Toff's mind, yet nothing about Draycott really surprised him.

The estate agent looked about thirty. He was as tall as Jolly but three inches shorter than the Toff. His shoulders were square and his grey coat fitted him well, although it was badly creased, as were his trousers; both gave the impression that they had been slept in. No one could have called James Draycott thin, but neither was he fat. A well-built, well-knit man, in good condition and with considerable physical strength; that was the Toff's estimate.

He had a likeable face – the kind of face which could explain Fay falling for him so suddenly and so completely. A homely face, yet in its way good-looking. His forehead was smooth, with the ruffled fair hair sticking up from it. His eyes were a cornflower blue, reminding the Toff of merry-eyed Pat Mullen of Mile Corner. His nose was short, a little blunt at the end, and his lips were full and well-enough shaped, with the upper lip short. His chin was aggressive and with a cleft, and just then covered with fair stubble.

Amongst other things, he needed a haircut

The Toff stepped in, and Jolly closed the door; and then Draycott and the Toff eyed each other, Draycott a little diffidently, and yet frankly enough, and the Toff smiling in a way which inspired trust in most men.

"Hallo, Draycott," he said. "I'm glad to see you."

Draycott hesitated as if in half surprise, and then he smiled; the smile was quick and merry, almost boyish, and yet clearly spontaneous; Draycott was that rare type, thought the Toff – a man who had no good idea of his looks or the impression he created.

"Well," he said, in a voice neither deep nor too high, "I suppose I ought to be glad to see you, too, Mr. Rollison. I've an idea that I am now. Your" – he looked at Jolly – "man has been giving me an outline of the story."

Jolly coughed.

"Mr. Draycott was a little restive, sir, and I felt it wise to entertain him."

Draycott chuckled, and took out a packet of cigarettes. The Toff accepted one as Draycott said: "Restive is right! He had to keep me quiet with a gun, and I was wondering what the chances were of throwing him out when he started to pitch his yarn. Sorry to put it like that," added Draycott apologetically, "but it does rather sound like one, doesn't it? I don't say I disbelieve *all* of it, but—"

"You can take it for gospel," said the Toff.

While Draycott looked at him sceptically, it seemed to the Toff that this was surely the most remarkable part of an amazing affair. There was Draycott, as cool and calm and casual as if he had not been hiding from the police on a charge of murder. Not far away McNab and Wilson would be making a complete inventory of the cottage; not quite so far away the unknown man was either unconscious or very uncomfortable in a ditch.

And Draycott was throwing doubt on Jolly's story!

"Well," said Draycott at last, "if it is, I'm sorry I've caused such a lot of trouble."

"Tell me," said the Toff gently, "has Jolly told you that the police are anxious to see you in order to prefer a charge of murder against you?"

Draycott stiffened.

"I don't believe that."

"It's true," said the Toff. "There was a body at your flat, and it started all the trouble."

Draycott pushed a hand through his overlong hair, stared, and said in complete bewilderment: "But this is nonsense! Jolly—you did say Jolly?—tells me that Ted Harrison had been with you some of the time. He knows better than that. I mean, I arranged with him to tell the whole story to the police. He told me the police considered I would be doing the best thing by staying under cover. It seemed crazy, but I'm not up in these things, and it's such a big affair that I wasn't altogether surprised. I—what are you looking like that for?"

The Toff was dwelling with bitterness on the duplicity of Ted Harrison: Harrison had known where Draycott was, and officially was liaison officer between Draycott and the police!

Chapter Twenty-Two

No Time For Talk

The Toff said in a far-away voice: "I'm looking like that because Harrison did take me in. I thought he was playing a minor role. However, it's as well I let him go. *If*," added the Toff slowly, "we can convince McNab that he's the liar and you're not."

"Who's McNab?" asked Draycott.

"At the moment your worst enemy," said the Toff, and explained. "Draycott, *were* you convinced that Harrison was helping you, and was in touch with the police? You'd no idea that he was double-crossing you?"

"I'd no idea, Rollison," Draycott said in a low voice. "If I had—" He clenched his fists. "I've been all kinds of a fool, that's obvious."

"Haven't we all?" asked the Toff. "How long will it take you to tell us just what you know is wrong?"

"Well," said Draycott, "about half an hour, I suppose; it's pretty complicated. But I've got to be sure that I ought to tell you first. He stepped to the window of the empty, dusty front room into which they had gone. "You can't expect me to take you entirely on trust. I've known Harrison for years—since we were at school—and I have no reason for thinking he would try to double-cross me." Draycott spoke quietly, and the Toff imagined that he was puzzling the situation out.

"Jolly, get outside and take the Frazer Nash a mile or two up the road, or the nearest point where you can hide it. If the Morris I've brought along isn't here when you get back," Rollison said, "make yourself scarce, because it means that McNab has finished with the cottage and is having a look here."

"Very good, sir," said Jolly.

If he was disappointed at the prospect of missing part of Draycott's story he did not say so. Draycott pushed a hand through his tousled hair and looked oddly at the Toff. "This *is* a bloody business."

"I couldn't agree more," said the Toff. "I'm going to give you a brief outline of the parts played by three people. Harrison—" he paused. "Miss Harvey is under arrest on, I suspect, a charge of being accessory after the fact to the murder you are supposed to have committed." He paused again, and Draycott gasped: "Phyllis under arrest!"

"Yes."

"I've never heard such nonsense in my life," said Draycott "She's no idea where I am, and—"

"You didn't tell her you were at Allen Cottage?"

"Of course I didn't. Only Harrison knew that. What are you trying to say?"

The Toff looked at him, himself so startled that he hardly knew what to say.

"I'm beginning to see," went on Draycott "Phyllis gave you my address, did she?"

"Yes."

"Thank God for that!" said Jimmy Draycott.

Afterwards the Toff said that of all the surprises he had received during this strange affair, that was the greatest. He had half expected an indignant denial that Phyllis Harvey could in any way be implicated, or at least a fierce defence of her – the kind of defence a lover would make before he had heard the full accusation. Alternatively a longer silence would not have surprised him. But Draycott had said: *"Thank God for that!"*

That was not the only surprising thing.

Until that moment Draycott had looked worried and anxious, except when the Toff had first arrived, but now seemed to smooth out the lines at his forehead and the frown; and he sat against the window-ledge, looking at the Toff.

"I suppose that sounds crazy too," Draycott said. "I'm not going to try to explain now, Rollison, except that—well, I'd always thought that Phyllis was wholly wrapped up in me. But if she told you she *must* have been involved in the business somewhere. In Harrison's confidence, I mean."

"That's likely," said the Toff. "When all's said and done, she thought him a friend of yours, and she would hardly be surprised if he passed on the information."

"You don't quite follow," said Draycott. "I'm working on the assumption that you've been telling me the truth, and Harrison's a liar and a rogue. And he wouldn't tell Phyllis where I was unless he thought she would let it out."

"Possibly not," admitted the Toff.

"And Phyllis believes I'm wanted by the police, yet she makes no attempt to get in touch with me, and—she lets you know. It's such a hell of a mess," said James Draycott, but he was smiling widely, as if it were nothing of the kind. "One *hell* of a mess, but it's going to let me out."

"Out of what?" asked the Toff, baffled.

Draycott said as if to himself: "My engagement, of course."

And even the Toff thought that was absolutely the limit; but a mental picture of Fay hovered in front of his mind's eye. He regarded Draycott for some seconds, then shrugged his shoulders.

"Well, you know what you know. And I know that in spite of what we've been saying this is no time for talk. Let's get out of here."

It was as well that they moved then.

They went out of the back door, and across a narrow garden chiefly remarkable for a large quantity of decayed cabbages, which smelt. At the bottom of the garden was a hedge some five feet high, untidy because it had not seen the shears for a long time. The Toff and Draycott reached it, and from beyond it they could see the cottage, both back and front.

McNab and Wilson were leaving the front door.

"We'll push the car," said Rollison. "They won't hear the engine."

There was a gravel path, wide enough for the small car and running the length of the garden. They pushed the Morris belonging to the man now in the ditch behind the hedge and sat in it. Through a gap in the hedge Rollison could just see the front gate of the bungalow.

McNab and Sergeant Wilson arrived, and the fact that they had a key to the bungalow proved that McNab had considered the possibility that he might find his quarry there. The Toff had looked about the floors and seen on them traces of dust, disturbed by footsteps which might have been made a week before. Only Draycott had smoked a whole cigarette, and the Toff had picked up the stub before leaving. There was no real reason why McNab should know that there had recently been occupants of the deserted bungalow.

They waited for twenty minutes, and then footsteps crunched on the gravel path. McNab said clearly: "We'll ask for a man from Winchester to watch the cottage, Wilson, but our bird's flown. Rolleeson will ha' warned him."

"Are you sure Rollison knew, sir?" asked Wilson.

"The mon always knows," said Chief Inspector McNab, with a hint of disgust.

Draycott eyed Rollison drolly, while the footsteps grew fainter along the path, and then echoed along the narrow road. Rollison opened the door of the Morris and stepped into the field behind the bungalow.

"That's that, for the moment. Are you convinced?"

"I am," said Draycott.

"Then McNab's done some good. I—"

Then the Toff stopped, while Draycott was half in and half out of the Morris, and also became quite still. From the corner of the hedge which they had not visited came a man's voice, low-pitched and yet reaching them clearly: "Put your hands up, both of you."

The Toff turned round, slowly, his hands as high as his shoulders, and he saw Harrison. The cricketer was standing with a gun in his hand, and with two other men, roughnecks both, by his side.

Harrison was in untidy tweeds, and his glasses were half-way down his nose.

Draycott snapped: "Put that down, you swine!"

"Don't let's waste words," said Harrison, "and don't shout for McNab. Rather than let them get you I'll shoot you both." It was clear that he meant what he said, and he did not look kindly: in fact in Harrison's somewhat ugly face there was a viciousness which startled the Toff.

Rollison said: "So you've come back."

"When *you* weren't expecting me," sneered Harrison. "You have been very much overrated, Rollison; you're nothing but a cheap imitation. Get back to the bungalow."

Draycott looked as if he would like to take a chance, but Rollison discouraged that with a shake of his head. One of the roughnecks led the way, and Harrison and the other followed them into the bungalow. By the door Rollison felt the muzzle of the gun in the small of his back. While it was there a roughneck ran through his pockets, and drew out the automatic he was carrying.

"That's drawn your teeth," Harrison said. "What did you do with Gort?"

"And who is Gort?" asked the Toff.

"So that's another thing you don't know," said Harrison. "The man who followed you here."

"He and a ditch are keeping company."

"So you can still be funny," snapped Harrison. He pushed the Toff so that he almost stumbled into the small kitchen of the bungalow. "Well, you won't be for long. I wonder what McNab will think when he finds your body as well as Draycott's?"

The Toff said easily: "He would certainly come to the conclusion that he was wrong about Draycott being the murderer. That won't help you."

"Don't be a bigger fool than you can help," said Harrison. "I'm fixing this so that Draycott shoots you, and then kills himself. He's going to write a confession, too. All about the way Harvey's wife was unfaithful, and got mixed up with Lorne and was blackmailed, and how Draycott killed the blackmailer and so on and so on. Convincing, isn't it?"

"McNab might think so," said the Toff. "But what is likely to happen while they look for you and Lorne?"

"Don't worry about us," said Harrison. "Lorne will be out of the country by tomorrow night, and I'm quite covered. In fact," he added suavely and looking at Draycott, "I'm going to get engaged very soon. I'll make Phyl a lot better husband than you, Jimmy. *And* I'll be the son-in-law of a very rich man. Oh, don't worry about me," said Harrison, and his voice rose a shade. "And you won't have time to worry about yourselves. Get in that corner, Rollison."

It was all so quiet, so callous. Rollison knew that he was very close to death, that Harrison would shoot him without a moment's compunction: Harrison was a far bigger rogue than he had dreamed, and to Rollison it seemed that he was to pay the penalty of underestimating an opponent. He thought of that in a detached manner, while he estimated the chances of besting Harrison in a rush at him. The chance was slim, but it was worth trying.

It was all so unreal and unnatural, and yet it was happening. There was no bluster, no histrionics, but simply a coldblooded plan for a double murder which was to look like murder and suicide, and so cover Harrison and others.

He saw Harrison lift the gun.

He tensed his muscles for a spring, but as he did so one of the roughnecks threw a chair at his legs. It caught him as he jumped, and he sprawled downwards.

Harrison swore, and: "You won't even go out quietly, won't you? Well—"

And he pointed the gun towards the Toff, who was lying on his back and quite helpless.

"Excuse me," said Jolly, in a very loud voice, and he made Harrison jump wildly.

Chapter Twenty-Three

Information From Draycott

Draycott moved then.

For some reason nothing had been done to stop him from moving, perhaps because he was not considered dangerous. But he jumped at Harrison, and made the man swing round. A bullet actually grazed his cheeks while he collided with Harrison and sent the man staggering into one of the roughnecks. The noise of the falling men, the smell of the shot, and the clattering of the gun as it fell to the bare boards all merged together, and as they came the Toff reached his feet.

He saw the only man not in the *mêlée* with a cosh in his hand, and ready to strike Draycott, reached the man and sent him reeling. Draycott was lying on top of Harrison, who was fighting viciously, while the second roughneck was picking himself up and reaching towards his left shoulder.

The Toff grabbed the chair and flung it at him. It struck his shoulder, and as the man fell back the gun at which he was snatching fell from his fingers. It hit the floor, but did not go off; and as Harrison's gun had been fitted with a silencer there had been no sound likely to travel as far as McNab and Wilson.

There was no sign of Jolly.

Draycott was getting the better of Harrison, and the Toff left him to it. One of the roughnecks was on his feet again, but he did not stay there long, for the Toff went in with vigour and ruthlessness. It might have been the narrowness of his escape from death, or it might have been just that he had reached the end of his patience, but by the time he had finished two men were unconscious, and the knuckles of his hands were grazed and raw. His hair was falling in his eyes, and he brushed it back impatiently, to see Draycott standing up and breathing heavily. Harrison was unconscious: judging from the purplish colour of his face, Draycott had almost strangled him.

"Well, that's that," Draycott said. "Thank God you're all right, Rollison."

"Thanks to you," said the Toff warmly. "You might dab at your cheek; it probably looks worse than it is, but it certainly looks nasty."

Draycott was surprised at the blood on his handkerchief, but the wound was little more than a scratch. When he brushed his fingers through his hair he dabbed blood on his forehead and on the fair strands, and the Toff smiled crookedly.

"You look the villain of the piece," he said. "Again—thanks more than I can say."

"Oh, *that*," said Draycott disparagingly. "You didn't expect me to let him shoot if I could help it, did you? Anyhow it was your chap. Wonder where he's gone. What are we going to do now, anyway?"

"We've four prisoners," mused the Toff, "and we want them kept nice and safe until we can convince McNab that he's talking through the back of his neck. On the whole, I should say this place is as well as any for keeping them."

"There's another bungalow—little more than a shed, really—half a mile across the fields," said Draycott. "It's in a copse of trees, and they'd be a lot safer there."

"We'll use it," said the Toff.

It was then that they stopped short, and looked sharply at each other, for they heard a stealthy sound outside. The Toff motioned Draycott towards the door with a quick nod of his head, and himself followed the man behind it.

The footsteps drew nearer and remained stealthy.

The Toff, with Harrison's gun in his hand, waited tensely while the door was pushed wider open: and then he heard a sharp exclamation, and: "Is there anything more for me to do, sir?"

Draycott drew in a sharp breath. The Toff stepped into full sight and regarded Jolly, who had looked away from the men on the floor and was standing in the doorway.

"What happened to you?" asked Rollison.

"I couldn't have arrived in time, so I shouted from a tree in the back garden," Jolly said. "Then I checked to make sure there were no others about."

"Jolly," Rollison said, "you have genius."

"Thanks." Almost without a change of tone he added: "Is the water on in this place?"

"I don't think so, sir."

"That's a pity, but we'll manage. How did you know there might be the need for stealth?"

While they bound the wrists and ankles of the prisoners Jolly explained that there was an old Buick behind the hedge on the left side of the bungalow, and that he had seen it as he had returned from parking the Frazer-Nash. He had approached stealthily in the hope of being useful, and he allowed himself to say that he had been considerably relieved when he had seen that Harrison and not the Toff was on the floor.

"You were not alone," said the Toff.

They did not waste much more time talking, but bundled the four men – after retrieving Gort from the ditch – into the Morris, which Jolly drove to the shed in the copse. Except the cottage and the bungalow there was no building in sight, and as the country about them was mostly gorse-land, and some miles from the village itself, there was little chance of anyone seeing them.

The Toff made arrangements quickly.

Jolly was to stay as jailer, and if he would have preferred a more active part he did not say so. The Toff and Draycott were to return to town, after dark, in the Morris – using that car because it would be less conspicuous than the Frazer-Nash.

"And how long shall I stay here, sir?" asked Jolly.

"I hope to release you tomorrow," said Rollison.

"Thank you. And if Harrison comes round, am I to endeavour to get his story?"

"Make him talk," said the Toff.
"*Very* good, sir," said Jolly, and he smiled.

* * *

For some fifty miles Rollison drove the Morris towards London, and Jimmy Draycott sat next to him, making occasional comments. They were near Staines when his self-restraint broke down, and he said with feeling: "You know, Rollison, you and that man of yours are freaks. Anyone would think that this was everyday business with you."

"That's very nearly true," said the Toff.

"Do you mean to say that all the stuff written about you in the Press isn't a lot of make-believe?"

"Oddly enough, there is crime other than that involving you, and I do play parts in it. However, I wouldn't like them all to take similar wrong turnings. I'm still hazy about this business. You can put most of it right."

"I *think* I can," said Draycott cautiously.

"I hope you can," said the Toff fervently. "First and foremost, they wanted to kill you."

"And don't I know it! That's why I hoofed it, although if I'd known Harrison hadn't given the police everything I certainly would have stayed. I don't think I've ever been so surprised about a man."

"Harrison can be left out for the moment. You heard the story he was trying to put over on the police, and it's remarkable that McNab had it off almost by heart. That suggests that McNab had been given an outline of the so-called mystery before. I don't like suggesting," he added thoughtfully, "that McNab has only contacted with Miss Harvey, but—"

Draycott said shortly: "It certainly looks like that. What is your opinion of her?"

"I think she allowed herself to be arrested, knowing—or believing—that no charge will ever be carried as far as the jury. Alternatively, I would say that she has been told to do it, and has obeyed because she can't help herself. I had the impression that she was using drugs. Her manner was too unreal to be natural, and too genuine to be assumed."

Draycott said: "I've thought she used drugs, for the last six months or so. She wouldn't admit it, of course, and—oh, Lord," exclaimed Draycott, "it is a hell of a mess! Back at the cottage I thought everything was working out, but if she's under the influence of drugs, and controlled by someone else as a result, I can't let her down."

"Meaning that you really would like to?"

"Like to!" exclaimed Draycott. "I—oh, damn it, I don't see why I should tell you, but you've a way with you. I've been wanting to get out of my engagement for a year. But she's had a bad time, what with her mother going off with people like Lorne—it wasn't the first *affaire*—and a pretty miserable home-life with her father, and her Aunt Charlotte ruling the roost, I hadn't the heart. And then the thing that really seemed to make it unavoidable happened. By 'it' I mean marrying her," added Draycott ingenuously.

"Meaning what?" asked the Toff.

"Well …" Draycott hesitated, and then said: "When it's all over she'll have to have help to recover."

Rollison said very slowly: "Your private affairs are nothing to do with me, but if you're contemplating marriage on those grounds you're in for trouble." They were driving along Chiswick High Street as he was speaking, but there was little traffic about. "You knew something that they wanted you dead for. Myra Harvey also knew it, and they killed her to make sure she said nothing—while she lived with Lorne there was no danger for her, but after the quarrel her murder was necessary." Draycott had heard the full story; he nodded, and waited. "Harrison acted as a go-between for the two parties. Harvey and Lorne. Lorne was the active partner, doing all the necessary dirty work. Harvey pulled the financial strings. You knew that there was a big-scale fraud in the offing. So did Myra Harvey."

"You're getting warm," Draycott said with a wry smile. "Only warm?" said the Toff. "Then we come to Phyllis Harvey. I'm assuming that she was and is drugged. Drugged, she did what her father told her. She came to me in order to lure me down to Allen Cottage, where you were hiding. I don't doubt that the idea was to kill us both and for you to leave a confession—forged, of course—to cover the murder at Grey Street as well."

"You're making Phyllis out a pretty bad lot," said Draycott uncomfortably.

"Possibly she did it only under threat. Certainly she tried to get me down to the cottage earlier than I went. But what *is* the game?" demanded the Toff. "I can work out the way it was being worked, I can easily see the careful establishing of a 'blackmail-cum-passion' series of crime, and have done so. But I don't know what is behind it." Draycott said: "I doubt if anyone in the world could, from your angle. I've known Mortimer Harvey for several years, and I was taken in for nearly six months. I stumbled across the truth by accident, and at first I couldn't believe what was happening. I got proof item by item, and then, like a fool, I confided in Harrison not knowing he was involved. Of course, that's why I was suddenly attacked—I was nearly killed when a car crashed into mine, and then shot at. I went into hiding. You see, I'd made notes from time to time and kept them on file in my desk. I meant to get Fay Gretton to find the file for me, but decided against it. I was afraid of involving her, and that's the last thing that I wanted to happen."

"Understood. Next?"

"Sorry," said Draycott. "It's so hard to believe. Er—Harvey was ill about a year ago. He went to France to recuperate, and—"

The Toff said, with a sudden hardness in his voice: "Oh, my Lord! And it's as simple as that!"

"So you've guessed," said Draycott quietly.

The Toff had guessed; and yet for several minutes as he drove along Piccadilly he could hardly bring his mind to believe it. The solution of the mystery was so simple, given the key, that it was incredible he had never thought of it. It explained Phyllis Harvey's addiction to drugs, and suggested she had not taken them in the first place willingly. It explained the need for the death of Myra Harvey, and it explained why Harvey himself had employed Lorne and his desperate gang of thugs to ensure that the truth did not get out.

But it *was* out.

"Ye-es," said the Toff very slowly, "I've guessed. Harvey *isn't* Harvey."

"That's right," said Draycott after a pause. "The man who came back from France was remarkably like him—even to mannerisms. I was taken in until I found that he didn't know much about the Mid-Provincial Building Society, from which he'd retired. When he lost me the agency it made me think even harder, and gradually I got the proof together. I'm not sure, but I think the man now calling himself Mortimer Harvey is a brother. I know Mortimer Harvey had one. It's going to be a devil of a thing to prove, though."

"Perhaps," said the Toff. "Perhaps. I—oh, damn, I've missed the turning!" He braked abruptly, backed a little, and then turned into Gresham Terrace. He drew up outside No. 55, his mind still revolting against the thing which he had learned and yet which seemed so incredible. And then his obsession was rudely shattered, for there were two cars standing outside No. 55.

One was Jamie Fraser's, and the other a large T-model Ford, by the side of which Bert of Mile Corner was standing.

The Toff braked, and opened the door. Draycott followed him to the pavement, while the Toff said to Bert: "What's the trouble?"

"Strike me, I 'ardly knows 'ow to tell yer," said Bert, and in the light from a street lamp it was clear that he was labouring under some strong emotion. "The dicks 'ave gorn from Gay Street an' Ma Kless's place, Mr. Ar."

"Well?" snapped the Toff.

But he did not get his answer then, for he heard a door open, and saw light streaming into the street. Running down the short flight of steps from No. 55 was Anthea, with Jamie on her heels.

"Rolly!" she exclaimed. "Rolly, thank God you've come! They've got Fay again. They—"

"Mr. Ar!" put in Bert urgently, "that's wot I've been tryin' to tell yer. They've took 'er to Ma Kless's. Arrived there an hour ago, she did."

And then, into the short silence, Draycott said: "If they hurt that girl I'll kill them. I'll kill each one with my bare hands."

It did not seem to the Toff an extravagant thing to say.

Chapter Twenty-Four

91 Gay Street

Had Draycott had his way they would have started for Gay Street immediately. The Toff decided against that, and reluctantly Draycott went with him upstairs. Jamie was in the lounge, while Bert followed Anthea, for whom he clearly had a keen admiration. He touched his forehead whenever she spoke.

Draycott was the first to speak.

"Rollison, if we know where Fay is, we're going there without losing a lot of time."

"We'll lose only the time that's necessary," said the Toff. "Rushing at it like a bull at a gate won't help us or Fay. I want to know when it happened and how," said the Toff. "And in the second we need a bite to eat, and some tea or coffee. And in the third," he added for Draycott's benefit, "we needn't worry a lot, since four of the men who have worked for Lorne are nicely tucked away, and the Kless brothers can't do much harm from the mortuary and the hospital respectively. We've got Lorne and Harvey to worry about"

"And Secretary Ramsey," said Draycott. "He was in the know. So was the woman—Phyllis's Aunt Charlotte."

"Aunt on whose side?" asked the Toff.

"Her father's. She's known about the change-over."

"*Could* we know what this is about?" demanded Anthea.

The Toff explained, while Anthea and Bert busied themselves in the kitchen, Bert apologising every time he managed to get in her way, and touching his forehead with surprising regularity.

Bert's two men had followed Fay from the office to Bays-water Road, and there had been no attempt to molest her. Soon after dark, however, the Mendoz brothers – on night duty – had been viciously attacked by two men, of whom Lorne undoubtedly was one. It had been characteristic that Tibby Mendoz, who recovered and was well enough to walk, had managed to get his brother into a taxi, and get back to Mile Comer, without advising the police. There he had told the story to Bert, who had hurried to Gresham Terrace.

Anthea had been with Fay in the drawing-room, and Fay had been tired, and dozing. Jamie had been out at his club. There had been a knock at the front door – opened by a maid – a scuffle, a cry, and then two men had burst into the drawing-room. Anthea had been thrust to one side, and silenced with a sack pulled over her head and shoulders and tied about her waist. She had not heard much struggling, although Fay had made a desperate effort to get to the window. That much Anthea had seen; but for the rest she could tell only of banging doors, a crying maid, another servant – a man – and then freedom from the sack, and realization that Fay had been kidnapped.

"Jamie wanted to go to the police, but I insisted on giving you until midnight," said Anthea.

"A touching faith," said the Toff slowly. He was eating sandwiches, and despite his impatience, Draycott was also eating and drinking. "I'm glad you did, Anthea. I don't think McNab or anyone else at the Yard realise what's at stake, and how desperately these people will act. Does anyone know," he added, "how much Mortimer Harvey is" – he said 'is' deliberately – "worth?"

"A million or more," said Draycott.

"High stakes indeed," said the Toff. "And don't ask me what the devil I'm going to do about it. Odd though it may seem, I've been thinking. Bert, attention!"

"Okay, Mr. Ar." Bert took his eyes from Anthea's fair face with reluctance, but made a thorough job of it this time. The Toff talked for some three minutes, and when he had finished Anthea said abruptly:

"That doesn't leave anything for me to do."

"It leaves you to be ready to welcome Fay when we get her back," said the Toff.

"I'm coming to Gay Street," said Jamie, as abruptly as his wife.

"I hope you won't insist," said Rollison. "You're to stay here with Anthea. If anything should go wrong the other end I'll need someone here to take messages."

* * *

In the small house, or more accurately hovel, which was 91 Gay Street, Mile End, a strangely assorted company was sitting in the larger of two upstairs rooms. Downstairs, in the passage and behind a door barricaded with boxes, chairs and a table, sat Ma Kless, a raddled old harridan with greasy hair, and lips which perpetually opened and closed as she sucked at the only three teeth that she retained. The only time she moved was to go into the filthy kitchen, the door of which was protected like the front door, and to empty from a filled pail a certain amount of water. This she replenished from a big kettle simmering on a low gas. The task finished, she would refill the kettle and put it back on the gas, and then carry the pail back to the hall, where the steam from the near-boiling water wafted in her face, so that it was beaded with moisture. She was wearing a grease-stained royal-blue dress; a thin, wiry, flat-fronted woman whose little eyes were filled with evil.

Upstairs, in a bedroom where there was a single iron bedstead and several kitchen chairs, were four people.

Fay was on the bed. She was lying full length, with a scarf tied about her mouth so tightly that her cheeks bulged above it. Her hands were also bound, but her legs were free. She had been lowered carelessly to the bed, and her skirt had rucked up so that it showed the tops of her stockings, and an inch or two of the white flesh above them. One shoe was off; the other made her foot and ankle look absurdly small. She was awake, and looking at the man nearest her. That was 'Mortimer Harvey', tall and too big for the chair, dressed in dark grey, and with a second-hand overcoat about him but not buttoned up. He was twisting a peaked cap in his hands, and his normally florid face had lost most of its colour. The cigar he was smoking had a pleasant aroma, but he was chewing it too much to get the best out of it.

Next to him was Ramsey, the wasp-waisted secretary Rollison had seen at the night-club. His hair was unruffled, but he kept smoothing it down nervously. The smoke from his Turkish cigarette was less attractive than that from Harvey's cigar.

The fourth member of the party was a majestic-looking woman with frizzy grey hair. The Toff had seen her at the night-club, and also at the house in Fulham, although he had not recognised her there. The sister of the real Mortimer Harvey had played a full part in the impersonation which had so nearly succeeded, as had Ramsey and – more unwittingly – Phyllis Harvey.

Phyllis was not there; nor was Lorne. Both Harvey and Ramsey kept looking towards the door, and their ears were strained to catch any sound. After what seemed an interminable silence Harvey said harshly: "You're sure Lorne was all right, Ramsey?"

"I assure you, sir, that he was quite well and free. He was contacting with Harrison in Winchester." Ramsey's manner was what it would have been with a genuine employer. "I'm sure that we shall be quite all right, sir."

"I never did think it was wise to come here," said Charlotte Harvey. "We'd be much better off at home."

"Don't be a fool," grunted Harvey. "We've got all the clothes we might want at the station, and the first place the police will visit if Rollison tells them anything is at St. John's Wood. No one would see us coming here, and we're quite safe."

"Then what are you sweating for?"

"Don't talk to me like that! If—if the police do get to the house Phyllis will stall them. God, I wish they hadn't released her yet. I—"

There was a noise from below stairs, and then a further sound of the barricade being taken away. Harvey stepped to the narrow landing, and from the dim light below he could see Ma Kless opening the door, and with the pail of water in her left hand. But she put it down, spilling a little over the edges, and admitted Lucius Lorne.

He pushed past her and hurried up the stairs.

When he reached the bedroom, and its better light, it was possible to see the pallor of his face, and the sweat on his forehead and his upper lip.

"Rollison got away," he gasped. "I saw him leaving Romsey in Harrison's Morris. He'll have been at his place for an hour now. When I get my hands on Harrison I'll strangle him!"

"Never mind about that," said Harvey, with an effort. "Go to the nearest telephone, Lorne. Call Rollison, and tell him that if the police come here we'll shoot our way out. And tell him we won't leave the Gretton girl alive."

Lorne said nervously: "I think we ought to get away while we can."

"Get that message out!" ordered Harvey. "We might do a deal with Rollison." He glanced across at Fay, as if reassuring himself that she was there, while Lorne went out.

A shadowy figure followed Lorne through the darkness.

The same shadowy figure watched him in the lighted telephone kiosk, but did not hear what he said to Rollison.

Lorne heard an easy voice, however, sweating profusely as he pressed the earpiece to his head.

"I've been expecting you," said the Toff, while at his side Draycott looked as if he wanted to snatch the receiver. "Get this clear. I'm coming to see you and to talk to Harvey, and when I know that the girl is all right we might come to terms."

Lorne said with an effort: "What—what kind of terms?"

"Harvey, so-called, is a very rich man," said the Toff very softly. "Remind him of that, Lorne, and remind yourself how unpleasant it would be on the gallows."

Chapter Twenty-Five

The Toff Makes Terms

As the Toff replaced the receiver Draycott stared at him with acute disapproval.

"Rollison, you're not going to make terms with those swine while I can stop it."

The Toff looked almost as if he had forgotten that he was there.

"You can believe me or not," he said, "but I am going to force terms on the whole crowd. If it's possible I'm going to make sure that no one is hurt. Including Fay Gretton. There is little honour among thieves, and there is no honour in me for Harvey and Lorne: I've simply made sure that they stay put until I reach them." Draycott drew a sharp breath.

"I didn't realise the way you looked at it. But aren't you going to tell the police?"

"Oh, yes," said the Toff, "I'm going to tell the police, and for McNab I'll dot the 'i's' and cross the 't's'. But not until after it's over. And please," said the Toff, moving towards the door and smiling at Anthea, "don't suggest that I ought to have the Yard with me when I go to Gay Street. If a rumour reaches them there that the police are on the way it's all up. They're quite desperate: from the start they've been ruthless."

"But need they know if the police are warned?"

"The whole of that part of Mile End might hate Ma Kless and whoever is with her, but if they've any quarrel with them they'll settle it their own way. Once there's a murmur of a concerted police attack on Ninety-one, word will reach the house. There's a kind of telepathy in the East End. The one quite vital thing, seeing that Fay's there, is to avoid the authorities. If Harvey and the mob were on their own it would be a different matter, and McNab could handle it with all the pleasure in the world. But we should be on the way."

Before he left he put on a waistcoat. They went first to Mile Corner, and saw Bert. Bert, still in his shirt-sleeves, looked forlorn, and a worried man. He was no longer smoking his pipe, but a bedraggled-looking home-made cigarette. He brightened a little when he saw the Toff.

"It's all ready, Mr. Ar—all the way you said."

"And the Mendoz brothers are safely away?"

"Like you said," said Bert, and it was clear that the Mendoz brothers were the reason for his gloom. "I never would 'ave berlieved it of them, Mr. Ar. *I'll* see they get what they need, don't *you* worry."

"Right," said the Toff. "Don't blame yourself, Bert. I'll be seeing you."

They walked towards Gay Street. Draycott would have been lost in the narrow streets, which ran like a rabbit warren in that strange quarter of London, but despite the darkness, illuminated only occasionally by flickering gas-lamps, the Toff went as surely as if he were walking along Regent Street.

"What's that about the Mendoz fellows?" asked Draycott. "Didn't you tell me they were working for you?"

"They were," said the Toff. "But they let Fay go twice, and they're first-class fighters. Clearly they didn't try to help her, and as clearly Harrison or Lorne got at them. But they won't have a chance to throw a spanner in the works this time."

"That's one good thing," said Draycott. "Rollison, what do you think are the chances of getting Fay out alive?"

"If you want the truth," said the Toff very grimly – "and I think you'd rather have it—there's a fifty-fifty chance."

They hurried silently through the darkness.

* * *

Ma Kless poured another kettle of steaming water into the pail, and took up her seat again behind the barricade of the door. Upstairs, the room where the main party was waiting showed a light that shone on the old harridan's greasy hair. The passage itself was unlighted, and the only sound was of the woman sucking her three teeth.

A footstep echoed outside.

Ma picked up the pail as the footsteps drew closer, and then there was a sharp tap on the door. Lorne came hurrying down, and reached her before she had finished clearing away the barricade.

"Get that water away!" snapped Lorne angrily. "I told you we were expecting someone, didn't I?"

"Yer never said 'oo, did yer?" The old crone's voice was harsh and ill-tempered.

"You do as your told." Lorne kicked away a plank of wood and then opened the door. As it opened the Toff came through, and on his heels was Draycott. He took in the scene in one swift glance, and as he did so Ma Kless screeched: "Yer bloody fool, that's Rollison!"

She lugged the pail up.

The Toff saw what was coming, and grabbed at Lorne and pushed the man towards the woman. The pail upset over Lorne's neck and shoulders, and he screamed with agony. A few splashes of the water fell on the Toff and Draycott, but did no damage, and the Toff reached Ma Kless. She was swearing viciously and kicking and hitting out, but he stopped her struggles with a grip at the back of her neck, then he gripped the seat of her skirt and carried her upstairs.

Harvey was at the door.

"Rollison, what are you doing?"

"Trying to stop this lady from being a nuisance," said the Toff. "She upset some hot water on Lorne. Draycott, watch Lorne," he called.

Then the Toff threw Ma Kless at Mr. 'Mortimer' Harvey, and as the big man dodged to one side, but failed to avoid her, the Toff went into the small room. He saw Fay on the bed, Charlotte Harvey standing over her with a gun, and Ramsey standing wild eyed by the wall.

The Toff went in, quite casually, reached Charlotte Harvey, who turned the gun towards him, and said sharply: "What kind of a deal is this? I thought we were coming to terms."

Harvey, breathing hard, and with a scratch on his cheek from Ma Kless's filthy nails, was just behind him.

"If you're trying to double cross me, Rollison, I'll see that girl's throat cut. If you're on the level, I'll give you ten thousand, and the girl, for a day's grace from the police. Come on, make up your mind."

As he spoke he took a knife from his pocket, and Ramsey showed a gun. The woman held her gun close to Rollison, while Ramsey stepped very softly towards Fay. Bound and gagged, she could only stare at the knife, which was no more than six inches from her eyes.

"When I talk about terms I mean terms, and not chicken feed," said the Toff. "If you say fifty thousand we might do a deal."

Harvey snapped: "Fifty thousand nothing! Why, you idiot, we can kill everyone of you. If you told the police where to find us we'd have heard by now, so you can't pull a bluff. Ten thousand, *and* the girl. That's my final offer. Have a look at *that,*" he added, and he looked towards Ramsey and Fay.

The Toff glanced quickly.

He had known from the first that the cold-bloodedness of those he was working against knew no bounds, and he knew also that Ramsey would use that knife if he were told. The older woman held the gun very steadily, a foot away from him.

Downstairs Lorne was moaning, and Draycott's footsteps sounded on the stairs. Outside the door Ma Kless was crouching, more like a beast than a woman, and she gibbered as Draycott came into sight.

"Make up your mind I" shouted Harvey.

Then, quite suddenly, a motor-horn sounded from outside. There was a long blast and a short one, and then silence. Harvey and the others started, but the Toff was unperturbed. Draycott entered by the door. At sight of the girl, and the man with the knife, his face drained of colour. He took a halfstep forward, but the Toff intervened.

"We've reached an agreement," he said. "Don't spoil it."

Then he moved towards the bed.

As he went Charlotte Harvey fired at point-blank range. The bullet struck him on the chest, high on the left side. He grunted, but it did not stop him; and the bullet fell to the floor! He struck at the woman, and kicked out at Ramsey. Ramsey lost his balance and fell across Fay, the knife striking against the wall and ripping paper and plaster from it. The Toff still went on, putting an arm about Ramsey and literally heaving him from Fay, while Jimmy Draycott hit the man who called himself Mortimer Harvey so hard that Harvey went sailing against the wall.

Ma Kless began to scream.

That screaming was nothing to the noise that suddenly began downstairs. Windows crashed and there was thunderous banging on the doors, back and front. While the Toff covered Fay, and twisted Charlotte Harvey's wrist so that she could not move, men stumbled into 91 Gay Street – Bert's men, led by Bert himself, men about whom no one would warn Harvey or the others. Ramsey picked himself up and made a rush for the door, but he fell into the arms of Bert, who simply shoved him back into the room.

"I got you, I saw it get you!" Charlotte screamed at Rollison.

"You forgot that I might be wearing a chain waistcoat," said the Toff. "I don't by habit, but at times it's wise. All right, Bert, we've got the lot."

"Nice work, Mr. Ar," said Bert.

The Toff untied the cords at Fay Gretton's wrists, and Jimmy Draycott unfastened the scarf about her face.

* * *

The police had a number of prisoners that night, and McNab heard a story which at first he was inclined to disbelieve; but finally he accepted it, chiefly because Charlotte Harvey broke down and confessed. The man who had called himself Mortimer Harvey *was* a brother, a renegade brother who had worked up the scheme a year before, and put it into operation when his brother had gone to the South of France to convalesce. Mortimer Harvey had died of natural causes, and his brother had taken his place.

Charlotte, Ramsey and Phyllis had had to know. Mortimer's son, Gerald, had been abroad and was not then a danger.

The first two had been willing partners, the sister because there was nothing for her in Mortimer's will, Ramsey because he received a good settlement. Phyllis also had acquiesced, but developed a conscience: and her relatives had complied with Lorne's suggestion that she should be drugged with cocaine.

But even that had not avoided trouble.

Draycott had found the truth, and Gerald Harvey had returned home. At first it was intended to murder Draycott and to make it look like suicide: then Gerald had complicated things, and he had been killed at Draycott's flat, so that Draycott should be accused of murder, *if* no way was found of killing him and presenting a suicide theory to the police.

Draycott, after two attempts on his life, had run for cover. Harrison had not worried, since he had known where to find him: but Harrison had kept that to himself, and not told Lorne or Harvey, chiefly – thought the Toff – because he wanted to do a little extra blackmail. To the Toff an astonishing thing was that Harrison had sent Fay to see him, yet it was explained simply enough: Harrison had been afraid that Fay would go to the police, and had thought it safe enough to send her to Rollison, whom he considered much overrated.

There was one other thing: Gerald Harvey had been murdered by Grab Kless, which explained that man's desperation in his attempt to get away from the train.

Altogether McNab was well satisfied, although he said that the Toff should have seen him about the raid. But he was grateful that he had been helped to avoid a major mistake, and the Toff left the Yard with McNab's blessing on him. He went to Gresham Terrace, where Fay and Anthea, and Jamie and Draycott were waiting. By then the police were on the way to Jolly and his prisoners.

But the Toff was not happy.

Nor, quite clearly, was Draycott.

There was a strange quiet in the lounge of the flat, and nothing to suggest a danger gone, and a triumph worthy of celebrating also past them. The Toff said slowly: "Well, Draycott?"

Draycott drew a deep breath.

"What can I do, Rollison? Phyllis has been drugged, she couldn't help herself. I've got to see her through this. I—I know I can rely on you not to tell Fay some—some of the things I said."

The Toff shrugged.

"If you want it that way, I'll keep quiet. But—"

He stopped, for unexpectedly the telephone rang; he lifted the receiver, and he heard Jolly's voice. He was at a Winchester hotel, and with Mr. Rollison's permission proposed to stay there for the night. But there was one thing which he felt he should report. From Harrison's pocket he had taken an interesting document. A marriage certificate, nearly a year old. The price of Harrison's part in the scheme – and he had been in it from the beginning – had been the hand of Phyllis Harvey.

The Toff said in a voice that positively echoed: "You mean she's married to *Harrison?*"

"Precisely, sir," said Jolly. "And I understand that the marriage was at first kept secret because it was feared that Mr. Draycott would learn of the deception, and that his devotion to Miss—er—Mrs. Harrison would ensure his compliance. I understand also, sir," said Jolly sonorously, "that the marriage was of her own free will, and some time before it was considered necessary to use drugs. Is that all you require tonight, sir?"

"It's more than all," said the Toff. "It's a miracle."

At first Draycott could not believe it, but soon Phyllis Harvey admitted it. She was very sorry for Jimmy. She had agreed to keep silent because she had not wanted to hurt him. She hoped he would forgive her, but she was very tired, too, and she wanted to sleep.

She would undergo a long course of treatment, and with luck she would recover. Long before that Lorne, Harrison, the renegade Harvey and Ramsey would be condemned, and Charlotte would be serving a life sentence, after a reprieve. And the thugs who had been with Harrison near Hurley would receive similar sentences.

While Mortimer Harvey's money was held in trust for Phyllis, which was as it should be.

Epilogue

Those were the things that came to the Toff's mind when he saw Fay Draycott at the New Forest cottage not a long way from Hurley. And he recalled the quiet registrar's office wedding some six months after the scene at Gay Street, and marvelled – as he had done at the time – that it was possible for two people like Fay and Jimmy Draycott to see each other and fall in love, and yet to keep silent, while the man remained faithful to a conception of things that included loyalty.

He recalled with some amusement that even after it was finished Draycott had wondered whether he had not indulged in something akin to a showy climax in his assault on 91 Gay Street No man who had not lived among the East Enders, and studied them for many years, would understand the paramount fact that against the police they were as one, even those who would have nothing to do with crime. Draycott would never fully realise that the first essential for the Toff had been to get into that hovel, and make sure that Fay was not hurt, and also that he had not dared to show a weapon, for that would have started the shooting match which he had wanted so desperately to avoid.

And had avoided.

There was one other thing they talked about: how Phyllis Harvey had recovered, and had gone to live in France. She was married to an American who admired her beauty as he would a picture; it was said they were very happy.

"And thank God they are!" said Fay. "Oh, what an impossible thing it seemed at one time, Rolly! And would have stayed that way, but for you. Don't say it wouldn't!"

The Toff smiled.

"I couldn't call it my greatest success," he said, "but I will call it the most interesting case I had met until then."

"You're better than Jolly at understatement," said Fay, pushing back her lovely hair. "How is he?"

"The last time I talked to him about you he had a complaint. He said that I had asked you for a list of the directors of the Mid-Provincial Company, and Murray and Firth, and that you forgot it."

"I didn't!" said Fay with spirit. "I had it in my bag when I was taken from Anthea's flat. I didn't worry about it afterwards, as it didn't matter."

"As I told Jolly," smiled the Toff, "but he insisted that it might have done. But now, Fay, I must be off."

He took his leave, waving to her until the cottage was out of sight.

John Creasey

Gideon's Day

Gideon's day is a busy one. He balances family commitments with solving a series of seemingly unrelated crimes from which a plot nonetheless evolves and a mystery is solved.

One of the most senior officers within Scotland Yard, George Gideon's crime solving abilities are in the finest traditions of London's world famous police headquarters. His analytical brain and sense of fairness is respected by colleagues and villains alike.

'The finest of all Scotland Yard series' – New York Times.

Gideon's Fire

Commander George Gideon of Scotland Yard has to deal successively with news of a mass murderer, a depraved maniac, and the deaths of a family in an arson attack on an old building south of the river. This leaves little time for the crisis developing at home ....

'Gideon of Scotland Yard emerges as one of the most real working detectives in modern fiction.... A sympathetic and believable professional policeman.' - New York Times

JOHN CREASEY

THE CREEPERS

"The prisoner's hand was thin and bony ... And in the centre of the palm was a pinkish mark. It was the shape of a wolf's head, mouth open, fangs showing. Although it was what he had expected to see, Inspector West felt a twinge of repugnance a stab not unrelated to fear. It was the fifth time he had seen the mark of the wolf – the mark of Lobo."

A gang of cat burglars led by Lobo cause mayhem as they terrorize the city. They must be stopped, but with little in the way of evidence the police are baffled. Just how can Inspector West manage to do this in what is a race against time before more victims succumb?

"Here is an excellent novel of law enforcement officers, harried, discouraged and desperately fatigued, moving inexorably ahead under the pressure of knowledge that they must succeed to save human lives." - Cleveland Plain-Dealer

"Furiously exciting" - Chicago Tribune

"The action is fast, continuous and exciting" - San Francisco News

JOHN CREASEY

INTRODUCING THE TOFF

Whilst returning home from a cricket match at his father's country home, the Honourable Richard Rollison - alias The Toff - comes across an accident which proves to be a mystery. As he delves deeper into the matter with his usual perseverance and thoroughness , murder and suspense form the backdrop to a fast moving and exciting adventure.

'The Toff has been promoted to a place of honour among amateur detectives.' – The Times Literary Supplement

CASE AGAINST PAUL RAEBURN

Chief Inspector Roger West has been watching and waiting for over two years – he is determined to catch Paul Raeburn out. The millionaire racketeer may have made a mistake, following the killing of a small time crook.

Can the ace detective triumph over the evil Raeburn in what are very difficult circumstances? This cannot be assumed as not eveything, it would seem, is as simple as it first appears .....

'Creasey can drive a narrative along like nobody's business ... ingenious plot ... interesting background .' - The Sunday Times